John Townsend Trowbridge

Two Biddicut Boys

And their Adventures with a Wonderful Trick Dog

John Townsend Trowbridge

Two Biddicut Boys
And their Adventures with a Wonderful Trick Dog

ISBN/EAN: 9783337177973

Printed in Europe, USA, Canada, Australia, Japan

Cover: Foto ©Andreas Hilbeck / pixelio.de

More available books at **www.hansebooks.com**

TWO BIDDICUT BOYS

AND THEIR ADVENTURES WITH
A WONDERFUL TRICK-DOG

BY

J. T. TROWBRIDGE

Illustrated

NEW YORK
THE CENTURY CO.
1898

CONTENTS

v

LIST OF ILLUSTRATIONS

vii

TWO BIDDICUT BOYS

TWO BIDDICUT BOYS

I

ON THE LAKE-SHORE

HE boys were putting on their clothes in the shadow of the ice-house, when a young man walking along the edge of the railroad embankment sauntered down to the shore, followed by a dog. He had on a narrow-brimmed, speckled straw hat and a loose sack-coat, and he carried a short stick in his hand.

He did n't seem to observe the boys, but the boys observed him.

"Looks like a lightning-rod man off on a vacation," said Cliff Chantry. "The one that rodded our new barn had just such a free-and-easy, I-own-the-earth sort of swagger."

"Bright-looking cur he 's got," said Ike Ingalls, tugging away at a stocking half-way on his wet foot.

"It 's an Irish terrier," said Dick Swan, hopping on one foot to jar the water out of his ear.

1   1

"That's no terrier," said the tallest of the boys, as he stood buttoning his shirt-collar, with his elbows spread, his chin up, and a prominent nose high in the air. "It's some sort of a spaniel; don't you see the ears?"—lowering his chin, and glancing in the direction of the dog and his master. "His legs are too long for any Irish terrier's."

"A spaniel it is, then; when Quint Whistler says a thing, that makes it so." Having uttered this sarcasm, Dick hopped on the other foot, to jounce the water out of his other ear.

Quint paid no attention to the taunt, but pulled down his wristbands under his coat-cuffs, and remarked dryly:

"What's that he's got in his hand?—I mean the man, not the dog. It's too big for a toothpick, but not big enough for a walking-stick."

"I'll tell you," suggested Cliff Chantry. "He's the leader of a band, and that's his band-stick. Don't you know?"—and he stopped combing his wet hair with his fingers, to make fantastic motions with an imaginary baton. "He's waving it now; see?"

"The dog's his band; he's waving it for him," said Quint. "There!"

The stick went splashing into the water a few rods from shore, and the dog went plunging and paddling after it.

"I knew he was a water-dog," said Quint.

"That's no sign," Cliff replied. "A terrier could do that. I'll ask him. I say, mister! what sort of a whelp is that?"

The young man waited until the dog brought him the

SPARKLER'S FIRST APPEARANCE.

stick, then turned to the boys coming down the slope and buttoning their last buttons.

"What sort of a whelp?" he repeated. "He's a sparkler. Did n't you ever see a sparkler?"

"Can't say I ever did," Cliff replied. "Never heard of one. What's a sparkler like?"

"As much like the animal you see here as your two thumbs are like each other. See him, and you see a sparkler. Hear him,"—at a motion of the stick the dog barked,—"and you hear a sparkler. Did you ever read Shakspere?"

"I know the dialogue between Brutus and Cassius, in the 'Advanced Speaker,'" Cliff replied. "I acted Cassius once, at a school exhibition, to this fellow's Brutus." He turned and looked up with a laugh at Quint Whistler, who was the last to come down to the shore, buttoning his vest by the way.

"Brutus,—Marcus Brutus,—this slab-sided chap with the gambrel-roof nose?" said the dog's owner, with a laugh which infected the whole crowd of boys, except Quint himself.

He had, as has been suggested, an exceptionally bold nasal protuberance; and there was a break in the high slope of it, somewhat suggestive of the roof in question. Cliff's nose, on the contrary, was short, but shapely, belonging to a frank, freckled, mirthful face—the face of a farmer's boy about sixteen years old. He was of medium height, and rather stocky. Quint was perhaps a year older, fully a head taller, lank of face and bony of frame.

His countenance was grave almost to sternness at this moment, as if he did n't altogether relish the personal nature of the young man's remarks.

The young man confronted the two, looking from one to the other with an air of lively satisfaction at having made their acquaintance. The boys' companions, half a dozen or more, gathered in a group, listening to the conversation.

"Brutus has got the most nose, but Cassius knows the most," the stranger rattled on gaily, "though it 's easier to decide about the nose than about the knowledge. If I could see you two act Brutus and Cassius, that might help settle the question."

Quint kept his frowning countenance, but Cliff answered laughingly:

"He 's great as Brutus! You should see him once! He used to step up on the teacher's platform to spout, 'When Marcus Brutus grows so covetous'; then when he got to,—'Be ready, gods, with all your thunderbolts! dash him to pieces!'—he would jump down on the floor with a jar that made the old school-house shake. Cassius was nowhere! But what has Shakspere, and Brutus and Cassius, to do with your pup?"

"That 's what I was coming to," replied the pup's master, holding the stick again, ready to throw. "In one of the plays is a heroine, 'created,' as her lover says, 'of every creature's best.' That 's what every fellow thinks of his girl, so it can't always be true. But it applies exactly to my dog. He is *multum in parvo, e pluribus*

unum, ne plus ultra. He 's a land-dog and a water-dog, a
sheep-dog and a watch-dog; as honest a dog as ever you
saw steal a sausage, and the cunningest trick-dog in the
wide world; as sly as a fox, and as amusing as a monkey.
Sparkler 's his name, and Sparkler 's his nature. Young
gentlemen, that paragon is for sale, and I invite you to
make an offer for him."

He threw the stick, and as the paragon went splashing
after it he added:

"What 'll you give, Brutus? Name a figure, Cassius!
Don't be bashful because I happen to be a stranger."

"I should n't think you would want to sell such a perfect creature as that," remarked Cliff Chantry.

"My young friend, you 're right. Nothing but dire
necessity could ever induce me to part with him. Necessity is a hard mistress; she 'll part a good boy and his
gran'ma, often a man and his money, sometimes a man and
his dog. Have you a silver half-dollar, Brutus? You,
Cassius, a quarter? I 'd like to flip it into the lake, for
you to see him paddle out and find it, dive to the bottom
for it, and bring it ashore. Anybody got a piece of bright
money?"

Brutus lifted his eyebrows at Cassius with a droll expression. Cassius drew down one side of his face with a
sagacious wink. The other boys likewise winked and
smiled, and two or three of them might have been observed to press their hands prudently on their pockets.
Bright pieces with which to strew the bottom of the lake
were not forthcoming.

"I am pained to perceive an air of incredulity among some of you," said the stranger.   "But to convince you—" He put his hand into his own pocket, and asked, "How deep is it out where he is now?"

"About up to your neck," said Cliff.

"That's all right.   This is the last quarter that remains to me out of a small fortune; but to show you the confidence I have in the sagacity of my four-footed friend— Here, Sparkler!"

Sparkler dropped the stick on the sand, put his nose to the coin, and yelped wishfully.

"Watch carefully!" his owner said to the boys.   "Look alive, Sparkler!"—and he flung the coin boldly out into the lake, where it sank in a circle of ripples.

The dog swam swiftly after it, put down his head into the clear water two or three times as he neared the spot, and finally went down altogether.   He seemed to be gone a long while: a few seconds seem a long while when you are watching a thing of that sort.

"I bet you he does n't bring up any silver quarter," said Cliff Chantry.

"How much will you bet?" cried the dog's owner, eagerly.   "Any fellow here wants to make a bet?   You, Brutus?   Put up some money, some of you!"

"But you 've no money to put up," said Quint Whistler.

"I 've that quarter—"

"At the bottom of the lake!" Cliff laughed excitedly.

"I 'll bet the dog!   The dog against a dollar!   That 's a hundred to one!   Quick!" cried the young man.   "There

he comes! Will you take the wager on what he's got in
his mouth?"

"I'm not in the habit of backing up my opinions with
bets," remarked Quint Whistler. "All is, I'm glad
't was n't my quarter you flung."

"He's got his mouth shut," said Ike Ingalls. "It was
open when he swam out."

"He's got a pebble in it! He's got his mouth full of
sand! Ho, ho!" The boys clamored and jeered, at the
same time watching with eager curiosity the dog paddling
shoreward.

"Boys," said the young man, gaily, "you are a squad
of young Solomons! You'll sling wisdom when you get
free from your mothers' apron-strings! Is n't that so,
Sparkler?"—as the dog came dripping out of the lake, and
dropped into his master's open palm, along with some
gravel, before the eyes of the intensely interested spectators, the recovered piece of money.

II

A ROMANTIC STORY

 "HAT 'S nothing to what he can do," said the young man, dipping the coin in the water and then wiping it with his handkerchief before returning it to his pocket. "Shake yourself, Sparkler!"

Sparkler shook himself, sending a shower of spray into the faces of the recoiling and backward tumbling boys. Quint Whistler alone stood his ground, receiving the drops on his nose with an equanimity that amused the stranger.

"Now I see what that gambrel-roof is for—to shed water. My object, young gentlemen, was not to get the water on to you, as you may perhaps imagine, but to get it off from Sparkler and reduce his weight by so much liquid; for now I am going to show you how he can jump. Sparkler!"

The young man held out the stick horizontally, about eighteen inches from the ground, and the dog leaped over it. He raised it six inches, and the dog went over it again.

So he kept raising it, and the dog continued to jump over it, until it was finally placed across the top of Ike Ingalls's head.

Ike shut his eyes, giggling nervously, and holding himself still, while the dog, just touching his shoulder lightly, went over the stick, and came down on the grass beyond.

"He 's a regular trick-dog," said the stranger. "Now, let me suggest a scheme. Brutus and Cassius will buy him for twenty-five dollars, and star the country with him. See ? Play Shakspere, and exhibit the dog! Can Mr. Whistler whistle ?" He had heard the boys call Quint by his full name. "Can either of you sing a comic song ? If you can, your fortune is made ! "

"I can whistle," said Quint, "like an empty jug; and we can both sing like a couple of cats on a back shed at two o'clock in the morning. But I 'm afraid that sort of whistling and singing would n't be popular, let alone our Shakspere ! "

Everybody laughed except Quint himself, who looked up with an appearance of mild surprise, as if to see where the fun came in.

"The dog alone will be attraction enough," said the stranger. "See what else he can do." He took off his coat and laid it on the grass. "Watch it, Sparkler ! "

The dog lay down beside it, with his paws on the collar.

"Now, would either of you young gentlemen like to earn a quarter ? If so, bring away that coat, and the lucre is yours."

"I don't care for the quarter, but I can get that coat,"

said Dick Swan, stepping carefully toward it, undeterred by the growls of Sparkler.

All watched with excited interest till he made a sudden snatch at it. But before his hand grasped the garment, Sparkler's teeth were fast in his sleeve—so fast, indeed, that as he sprang back he left a piece of his cuff in the dog's mouth, amid the loud laughter of his companions.

"He can do a hundred things," said the stranger. "Here's one."

Beside his coat on the grass he placed his handkerchief; beside that he laid his stick, and near that the silver quarter; then over the quarter he turned his hat.

"Now, boys," he said, stepping back a few paces, "which of those articles shall he bring to me?"

"The handkerchief," said Cliff.

"You hear, Sparkler," said the master; "the handkerchief."

And without hesitation the dog picked it up and brought it to him.

"Now, Brutus, what will you have?"

"I say the thing that's under the hat," Quint replied.

"Very well; the money that's under the hat," said the master. Whereupon Sparkler tipped the hat over with his nose, nipped daintily at the coin, which he took up, along with some grass, and dropped into the young man's extended hand.

"That's judgmatical!" said Quint.

And Cliff exclaimed: "He's great! Why don't you exhibit him yourself?"

"That 's what I am doing at this moment," said the dog's owner; "and that 's what I 've done to hundreds of delighted spectators. Sparkler never fails to sparkle. But to pass around the hat—that 's another question. If I 've a weak point, it 's my modesty."

"Your modesty is as plain as a gambrel-roof nose," said Quint Whistler, solemnly.

"Brutus," said the young man, laughing good-naturedly with the rest, "we 're even. You owed me one, and you have paid it." He put on his coat, and proceeded: "I am the son of a distinguished lawyer, lately deceased; and I am now on my way to the bedside of a sick mother in Michigan, who has sent for me without knowing that I have no money for the journey."

Cliff fondled the dog's wet head, and inquired: "How do you happen to be out of money so far from home?"

The young man pulled down his cuffs under his coat-sleeves, and smilingly answered:

"That 's a long story, but it can be briefly told. I was employed as clerk in the big hotel in Bennington—the Stark Hotel, which was burned two weeks ago. What! you did n't hear of that big fire? Well, you *would* have heard of it if you had been in town that night. 'T was a clean sweep! Inmates lost about everything—barely escaped with their lives. I was so busy getting out the hotel books, and helping the women and children, that I could n't give any time to my own personal effects; so I lost all my clothing, except what I had on my back, and all my books and private papers. I had some money in my pocket; but

I 've spent that, waiting to get my back salary of the proprietor. He owes me seven hundred dollars; but I could n't get it, because he had n't settled with the insurance companies. I was lucky in one thing—I saved my dog. I threw him from a three-story window."

"Seems to me that 's a three-story kind of a story," observed Quint.

"Wait till I tell you," said the young man, not at all disconcerted. "This was twelve o'clock at night. Think of it! He saw I was in danger—would stick to my heels, you know, while I was rousing the guests; he really helped me, by barking up and down the corridors, till I tumbled a feather-bed out of a window, and dropped him on it."

"I don't see how you *can* part with him!" Cliff exclaimed, caressing the wonderful quadruped.

"Necessity—sheer necessity!" answered the young man. "To be perfectly frank with you, I shall sell him conditionally, if at all, with the privilege of buying him back, at double the price, any time within three months. Give me twenty-five dollars for him, and if I don't pay you fifty within ninety days, the dog is yours. I 'm willing to put that in writing."

"I have n't got twenty-five dollars in the world," said Cliff, his eyes glistening with excitement as he looked appealingly at his companions, "and I could n't raise so much."

"How much can you raise?"

"I don't know."

Cliff walked aside with Quint, two or three others following.

"You don't really think of buying him, do you?" said Ike Ingalls.

"I would, in a minute, if I could," said Cliff. "He's just wonderful! Say, Quint, what do you say to going in with me?"

"I'm afraid 't would n't work well for two boys to own one dog," replied Quint; "but I should like to see you own him, and I'll lend you a little money, if you like."

"Will you?" said Cliff, eagerly.

"Yes; but let me give you something else first: that's advice. You are worked up now; you are more excitable than I am. You'd better wait till you've had time to think it over and ask your folks. You want to do a thing like this when your head is cool."

"My head is cool enough," said Cliff. "But, cool or hot, I want that dog! As for my folks, I know they would n't consent, if I should ask them. But if I take him home, show his tricks, and let on by degrees that I've bought him conditionally, to double my money when the owner comes for him,—if he ever does come: I shall hope he won't!—I don't think they'll say much."

"Well, you know best about it," said Quint. "I've got four or five dollars at home I can let you have."

"I can lend you three dollars," Ike Ingalls whispered, eager to see the trade go on.

Dick Swan offered to advance two more, likewise inter-

ested in seeing so wonderful a dog brought into the neighborhood.

"Now, don't you appear too anxious!" Quint warned
his enthusiastic friend.

"Oh, no!" said Cliff, with flushed cheeks and suffused
eyes.   "I 'm as cool as a cucumber in an ice-house!"

III

HEN the friends went back to where the dog was, they found him sitting up in a comical attitude, with his fore paws pointing at the handkerchief, thrown over the top of the stick, which was stuck in the turf.

"He feels a little chilly after his bath, and he is warming his hands," his master explained. "You may think it's rather a cold fire, but that's nothing to a dog that has a little imagination. Don't burn your fingers, Sparkler!"

The dog actually drew his paws back a little, showing his teeth and winking with his pleasant brown eyes, as if he enjoyed the humor of the situation.

"That will do; now put out the fire."

The dog pulled the handkerchief from the stick, and put his paws upon it.

"You see what he is," cried the owner, turning to Cliff. "What do you say?"

Cliff was more than ever determined to possess so

17

marvelous a creature. But keeping in mind his friend's caution, and remembering how he had seen shrewd jockeys swap horses, he assumed an indifferent air, and answered diplomatically:

"I can't raise the money; I told you before."

"How did you come by the dog?" Quint inquired.

"That's a part of the story I believe I did n't tell," replied the young man. "He was a puppy one of the hostlers had in the hotel stables. I saw there was good stuff in him, bought him for a six-bladed jack-knife with a cork-screw and a gimlet, and gave my leisure time to training him."

Quint stooped to look at the dog's collar, and remarked that it bore no name or number.

"Has he ever been licensed?" he inquired.

"Licensed? Yes," said the young man, with a smile of amusement at the simplicity of the question. "But in country places, where every dog is known, the law requiring names and license numbers on dogs' collars is apt to be a dead letter." He turned to Cliff. "How much *can* you raise?"

"I can raise five dollars; I'll give that for the dog," said Cliff, with a composed expression (such as he had noticed on the faces of horse-traders), but with a wildly throbbing heart.

The owner regarded him with a sad and pitying smile.

"I gave you credit for being a well-intentioned young man," he said; "and I supposed any one who had ever taken the great part of Cassius would have too high an

appreciation of good acting to make such an offer for such
a performer as my dog Sparkler. Why, sir, it would make
him blush—it would make him hang his head for shame
—to be sold for a paltry sum like that!"

It certainly made Cliff ashamed, to have the pettiness
of his offer held up to contempt in this way, and he
would have blushed, if his face had n't been so very red
before. He murmured something about having no more
money.

"But your friends will lend you some; I see it in their
eyes. Now, I 'll tell you what I 'll do. I believe you 'll be
a kind master; and I saw, when you were stroking him,
that he had taken a liking to you. He knows a good dog-
lover when he sees one, and he picked you out of the
crowd. Give me twenty dollars, and the privilege of buying him back at forty, and he 's yours."

"I 'll give you ten," said Cliff, quickly. "That 's all I
will give."

The other boys looked eagerly from his face to that of
the young man, in which they saw signs of relenting. As
Cliff could n't be moved to raise his offer, the owner finally
said:

"And I hold the right to buy him back?"

"Yes," replied Cliff, "at double the price."

The young man laughed, and shrugged.

"On the whole," he said, "I think that will be as well
for me. I shall save money when I come to reclaim him;
and the ten dollars will take me as far as Buffalo, where
I have friends who will help me over the rest of the jour-

2

ney. I would n't have sold him outright, if you had offered
a hundred."

He took a small cord from his pocket, which he made
fast to the dog's collar.

"This is hardly necessary," he observed, "for if I tell
him to go with you he will go; but it will be safer to place
him under some restraint until I get well out of the way.
I shall hurry down to the Junction, and take the first west-
bound train." He stood ready to put the loose end of the
cord into Cliff's hand. "Now, where 's your ten dollars,
young man?"

"These boys are going to get it for me," said Cliff.
"They live nearer here than I do. You 'll give me a bill
of sale?"

"Certainly, if you require it. Hurry up, and I 'll wait
here."

Some of the boys went with Cliff and Quint, while the
rest remained in the delightful company of the performing dog and his master. In a short time those who had
departed came running back, Cliff at their head, and Quint
lagging in the rear; and Cliff, out of breath, paid with
trembling hands his borrowed money. He received, in
return, the end of the cord, and a leaf torn from the
stranger's note-book. On this was penciled a memorandum
of the transaction, signed "A. K. Winslow."

"My usual signature," said the dog's late owner,
"though I may as well tell you that the A. stands for
Algernon and the K. for Knight, and that my address will
be Battle Creek, Michigan, till further notice. That is

your receipted bill, with the redemption clause inserted. Now here is something for you to sign."

He held out his open note-book, in which Cliff read, on a penciled page:

"Purchased of A. K. Winslow, for ten dollars ($10), his trick-dog Sparkler, which I agree to re-deliver to him, or to his order, on the payment of twice that sum ($20), any time within three months."

This, like the bill of sale, was duly dated; and Cliff, after consulting with Quint, who thought it "judgmatical," gave it his signature.

"I keep this, you keep that, and these friends of yours are our witnesses," said Algernon Knight Winslow, in the best of spirits, notwithstanding the present necessity of parting from his four-footed companion. "Sparkler, look alive!"

The dog sat up, with fore legs lifted, while his late master addressed him, with one forefinger pointed impressively:

"Sparkler, sharer of my fortunes, will you go with this young gentleman who holds you by the cord, stay with him faithfully, serve him obediently, and perform tricks for him as you would for me, till I send or come myself to claim you? Answer!"

Sparkler regarded him with half-closed, sleepy-looking eyes, and dropped one paw.

"That means yes," said Algernon K. Winslow. "And now you have him."

"You don't mean to say he takes in all you 've been saying?" Cliff queried wonderingly.

"He takes in the gist of it as well as either of you. Now, with regard to his tricks"—and Mr. Winslow went on to give Cliff some useful hints on that all-important subject.

The dog was never to be whipped under any circumstances, but always to be treated kindly, and rewarded with nice bits from the table after each performance.

"And I advise you to feed him as soon as you get home; for he has been on rather short allowance lately. Now, good-by! Farewell! Adieu! Au revoir! Till we meet again!" cried A. K. Winslow, gaily.

Cliff had still some questions to ask regarding the tricks, which being obligingly answered, he said, "Come, Sparkler!" and set off, cord in hand, accompanied by the dog, that went as readily as if he had been acting one of his well-understood parts.

Cliff was overjoyed; and his friends, running beside him and the leashed animal, were almost as jubilant as he. Next to owning a trick-dog is the pleasure of having a friend own one.

"By-by!" Algernon K. Winslow called after them, waving his hand, as he turned and walked smilingly away.

IV

CLIFF BRINGS HOME HIS PURCHASE

"AND'S sake alive! What's up?" ex claimed Mrs. Chantry, looking from the window of the old Chantry farm-house, and seeing a rabble of boys, headed by her son Clifford, leading a strange dog, turn in at the gate.

On their way through the village the original party of six or seven had been joined by other boys, eager to hear about the dog; and now two more, younger brothers of Cliff, ran out from the barn to meet the astonishing procession.

"What ye got there? Where'd ye get that dog?" cried the younger brothers (aged twelve and ten), almost with one voice.

"Bought him!" replied Cliff, walking proudly on, followed by his rabble.

"Who of? What did ye give? What's he good for?" clamored the younger brothers, falling into the ranks.

"He's a trick-dog, and he's worth a hundred dollars!"

23

said Sparkler's new owner. "Now just keep quiet, and let me get him tied up in the woodhouse before you scare him to death. I'll tell you all about it in a minute, ma!" he cried, passing on to the rear of the house, regardless of his mother's expostulations.

She intercepted him at the back door.

"Tell me now! Stop right where you are!" she commanded him. "Have you been buying a dog without permission from your father or me?"

"I did n't have time to get permission; 't would n't do to let such a chance slip. He 's just the knowingest dog you ever saw or heard of. You and pa will both say it 's all right when I tell you," said Cliff, leading his prize and his mob of boys into the woodshed—a barn-like addition to the house, with one large door opening into the back yard, and a smaller one within communicating with the kitchen.

"The boy 's out of his head!" Mrs. Chantry exclaimed. "I should think they had all broken out of bedlam. Amos and Trafton have run wild with the rest. Where are *you* going, Susie?"

"I want to see the dog," said Susie, a fourteen-year-old sister of Cliff's.

"I declare, you 're crazy too! Did n't anybody ever see a dog before?" cried the mother, impatiently, but not ill-naturedly, for she was one of the indulgent sort. "Run and find your father, and tell him if he does n't want his woodhouse turned into a pandemonium, he 'd better come quick!"

Having got Sparkler into the woodshed, and fastened him by his cord to the leg of a grindstone, Cliff told his brothers they might "just stroke his ears a little," but not to "fool with him," and charged Quint Whistler to look out for the other boys, who were crowding around; then he went bustling into the kitchen, calling out:

"What can I feed him? Say, ma, what can I give my dog to eat?"

"That's a strange how-d'e-do!" Mrs. Chantry exclaimed; "before you 've told me what dog it is, or how you came by him! As if I was your servant, to feed any stray creetur' you choose to bring into the house!"

"He is n't a 'stray creetur''!" cried Cliff, "and I don't ask you to feed him; I 'll do that myself. The man I had him of said cold chicken was particularly nice for him."

He was already on his way to the cellar, where the cold victuals were kept.

"Precious little cold chicken he or any other dog will get in this house!" his mother called after him from the head of the stairs. "And don't give him too much of that cold roast veal, either! I want enough left to hash up for breakfast. Be sure and shut the cover tight. The idee of bringing in a hungry whelp to eat us out of house and home!"

"What else is there?" cried Cliff from below, his voice sounding hollow and distant, as if he had his head in the ice-chest.

"Maybe he 'll eat a cold potato, or some bread soaked in milk. Most dogs like bread and milk."

She handed down a plate and a knife, which Cliff reached up for from the stairway; and, having relieved her feelings by scólding him for his folly, she afterward helped him prepare a bountiful repast for Sparkler. She even showed her interest in his strange purchase so far as to go and stand in the doorway that opened from the kitchen into the woodshed, and see the "stray creetur'" fed.

There she was found by Susie, returning from the errand to her father.

"You are not going to be crazy too, are you, ma?" said the girl, mischievously.

The good woman's countenance, which she endeavored to keep severe, beamed with kindness and curiosity.

"Law, no, child!" she said; "but I want to see that good victuals ain't wasted. I don't wonder you are surprised, father!"

"Father" was the father of her children—a sturdy, red-faced farmer, with a shaven chin hedged by long side-whiskers, who had just appeared at the outer door of the woodshed. This door had been shut to prevent the possible escape of the dog; but he opened it to the width of his broad shoulders, and looked in with a scowl of humorous amazement.

"What's all this?" he demanded. "I should think Barnum's 'Greatest Show on Earth' had emptied itself on my premises!" Over the heads of the smaller boys he saw tall Quint Whistler standing by the grindstone, keeping back the crowd while the dog ate. "That your dog, Quint?"

"No; I don't own so much as a wag of his tail. Wish I did!" said Quint.

"He's got a mortgage on him; so have I," said Ike Ingalls. "He's a trick-dog, and a buster!"

Just then Cliff got up from the floor, where he was kneeling by the plate, in rapturous satisfaction at the way its contents disappeared down the dog's throat.

"He's my dog," he said, turning only the side of his flushed face toward the outer door, without venturing to look at his father. "He's been trained to do almost anything. There's no end to the tricks he can perform. And he's a good watch-dog. Look at Dick's coat-sleeve! He got that tear trying to pull a coat away from him after he had been told to guard it."

The mouth between the long side-whiskers worked with grim humor, and said sarcastically:

"There seems to be another thing he can do pretty well —dispose of a plate of victuals! Did you pick him up in the street?"

"No, I did n't. You can't pick up such dogs as this in the street, nor anywhere else," Cliff replied, with spirit.

"He bought him," spoke up his younger brother Amos, his face in a broad grin.

All eyes turned again to the father in the doorway, who gave a tugging pull at the fleece of his left whisker, and exclaimed:

"You did n't pay money for a mangy cur like that, I hope!"

"He is n't a mangy cur!" Cliff declared indignantly.

He did n't know just what "mangy" meant, but inferred
that it must be something discreditable.   "He 's just as
nice as he can be.   I *had* to pay a little money for him—
a very little; but you won't blame me when you see the
kind of dog he is.   I have n't bought him outright, either;
I expect his owner will come for him, and pay me well for
his keep, inside of three months.   Here, ma, take the plate.
He has licked it clean of everything but the cold potato.
Now, stand a little farther off, boys, and I 'll show you his
tricks."

V

THE ORIGIN OF THE WORD "DOGGED"

SPACE was cleared for the first exhibition of Cliff's wonderful trick-dog. Some of the spectators climbed upon the piled wood; one stood on the frame of the grindstone, another on the chopping-block, two or three sat on a board placed across the tops of empty barrels, and the rest of the boys filled up the ring.

In the midst stood Quint Whistler and Ike Ingalls, in the distinguished capacity of Cliff's counselors and assistants—thus favored because they had advanced money for the purchase. Dick Swan's mother had refused to let him lend his money, greatly to his disappointment; but he had the next place, on account of the good will he had shown.

In the kitchen door stood smiling Mrs. Chantry, with Susie clinging excitedly to her elbow. Amos and Trafton were on the steps below. The father's broad shoulders and straight-brimmed straw hat were defined against the after-

noon light in the partly opened woodshed door, the sarcastic smile still playing about his mouth.

Cliff held in one hand the end of the cord, which he had
detached from the leg of the grindstone, and in the other
a thin stick of pine kindlings. At his feet was the dog,
couched on his paws, with his tongue out, looking com-
placent after his meal.

"Make him jump the first thing," said Ike Ingalls, proud
of his part in the show. Then, turning to Mr. Chantry:
"He can jump over my head; he did it down on the
shore."

"Get up, Sparkler!" Cliff commanded.

Sparkler lolled, without stirring from his comfortable
position.

"Say 'Look alive,'" Quint suggested in a low voice.

"Look alive!" Cliff repeated in a tone of authority.

As the trick-dog still showed no disposition to obey, he
gave the cord a jerk which brought him to his feet.

"Now jump!" he said, holding his stick about eighteen
inches from the floor, while Ike Ingalls made the nearest
boys take a step or two backward, to give ample room for
the leap.

But it was a useless trouble. Sparkler never moved.

"You hold it too high, to begin with," said Quint.

So Cliff lowered the stick a few inches, and again commanded: "Jump, now!"—with no better result.

"Lower yet!" whispered Quint.

Cliff did so, and repeated his commands, at the same
time jerking the cord to rouse the wonderful trick-dog

from his indifference. But Sparkler only lolled and looked stupid.

"Lay the stick on the floor," said the whiskered face in the doorway. "Maybe he 'll walk over it."

The spectators began to titter. Cliff, confused, covered with perspiration and blushes, pulled the cord, and knocked the dog's paws with the stick, repeating sharply, "Jump, I say!" But Sparkler hung back.

The mother's face wore a look of disappointment, and of pity for her son's humiliation. But the whiskered visage in the doorway was wreathed with ironic smiles.

"He *can* jump, but he won't," said Ike Ingalls. "He 's balky."

"He 's showing us the origin of the word 'dogged,'" said the amused farmer.

"He did n't like it because you yanked him by the cord," Quint Whistler argued. "Don't you remember, his owner said you must never be rough with him?"

"I did n't think I was rough," Cliff replied.

He found a handkerchief somewhere in his pockets, and wiped his forehead, still looking down, with a face of perplexity and disgust, at the disobedient beast.

"Another thing he said, too, which I 'd forgotten," Quint proceeded: "he said he must be fed after a performance, not before. You could n't expect him to jump after a full meal."

"That 's so!" Cliff assented, with a long breath.

"Try making him sit up," said Dick Swan.

Cliff was averse to the attempt, in the present state of

the canine appetite; but as Dick's suggestion was clamorously backed up by the crowd of boys, and there was still a possibility of the dog's redeeming his sunken reputation, he stroked and coaxed him, and finally, remembering the late owner's word and gesture, threw up the hand that held the stick, and cried out cheerily:

"Look alive, now! Look alive, Sparkler!"

Sparkler looked anything but alive; on the contrary, he looked quite asleep as he stretched himself out, closing his languid eyes, by the leg of the grindstone.

"What a wonderful dog! Oh, Cliff!" jeered the boys who had previously been most envious of his purchase. "Why don't you brag some more about him?"

"There, there, boys! don't make fun," said Mrs. Chantry. "And don't feel bad, my son. The best of us are liable to be deceived in a bargain."

"Say, Cliff! how much did you give?" asked his brother Amos.

The father laughed pitilessly.

"If he gave ten cents, he got swindled," was his cruel comment. "Now, quit your nonsense, and come and help me mend the pig-pen. When I said you could go in swimming, I did n't expect you to bring home a beggarly pup to fool with all the afternoon."

Cliff stood for some moments with bent brows, eying the "dogged" dog with extreme discontent. When he raised his head, his father's unwelcome face had disappeared, and his mother had drawn Susie back into the kitchen. The crowd was beginning to disperse, some

"THE THREE DOLLARS AND A HALF I LENT YOU—'"

laughing as they went, others lingering to hear what Cliff
would have to say.

One lingered from a different motive; that was Ike
Ingalls.

"If you 'd just as lieves pay me the three dollars and a
half I lent you—" he began in a low voice, at Cliff's ear.

Cliff turned upon him a scornful scowl.

"I 'll pay you so quick it 'll make your head swim!" he
exclaimed, loud enough for all to hear. "You were glad
enough to lend it and help me buy the dog, and you felt
easy enough about it till you began to think I 'd been
cheated. Ame, go up to my room and get my money-pouch
out of the till of my chest; and say nothing to anybody."

"Don't mind about paying me," said Quint. "I would n't
ask for my money if I knew you 'd bought a worthless
dog; but I don't believe you have. You could n't expect
him to perform tricks in a crowd of strangers, before he 'd
got well acquainted with you."

"No; he has n't got used to his new master," said Dick
Swan, encouragingly. "I would n't come down on you
for *my* money, would I? I 'm sorrier 'n I was before, ma
would n't let me lend it to you."

"*You* 're all right, Dick; so is Quint," Cliff replied, his
brows clearing. "So am I! I don't give him up as a bad
job—not yet! His dinner made him logy; that 's what 's
the matter. Then again, father looking on, the way he
did, made me nervous. I knew he was just waiting to
laugh at me. Ten cents!" the boy repeated, with a dis-
mal laugh.

"You never must be nervous when you are training an animal," Quint remarked. "That's so with horses, and it must be so with dogs. He'll come out all right, I know! If he does n't, you need n't pay me back more than half my money; for it was partly my fault, your buying him."

"By Jehu, Quint!" Cliff exclaimed, with a burst of grateful feeling, "you are a whole load of bricks! But I shall pay you every cent, all the same—sometime, if not to-day. Give it here, Ame"—to the boy bringing the pouch.

Cliff untied the string, and began to count out silver half-dollars. Ike, meanwhile, feeling that his eagerness to receive back his loan contrasted unfavorably with Quint's more generous conduct, and with what Dick would likewise have done in his place, looked furtively around for evidences of his own waning popularity on the faces of his companions.

"Here, Ike!" said Cliff, jingling seven half-dollars in his extended palm.

Ike was conscious of a chilly social atmosphere surrounding him; but he was nevertheless glad to see his money again.

"I did n't want you to think I was in any hurry for my pay," he said, as he reached out his hand for it. "I thought—"

"That's all right, Ike," said Cliff, without any show of resentment. "I can give you a part of yours, Quint—"

"No; leave it now," replied Quint; "or—just as you say." And, Cliff insisting, he took the last of the silver which Cliff withdrew from the pouch. "Now don't worry about the rest; let it go till—what 's his name?—A. K. Winslow buys back his dog," he added, with a droll smile.

"Not a word, boys, about this money," Cliff cautioned his brothers. "I prefer to tell father myself. Now, fellows, I 've got to shut up here. Sorry to turn you out, but"— tying the dog's cord again to the leg of the grindstone— "father wants me, and I 'm going to leave Master Sparkler to meditate on his disgraceful conduct."

Having got the last of the boys out of the woodshed, and shut the large outer door, he beckoned Quint to remain, and said to him confidentially:

"Can't you come around this evening? When everything is quiet, and he has digested his dinner, I am going to try him again, and see if he 'll do his tricks any better on an empty stomach."

VI

"DID N'T I TELL YOU SO?"

HILE the two were at work repairing the pig-pen, Mr. Chantry forbore to ask any questions regarding the "beggarly pup" his son had brought home.

"What he has to say about that will keep," Cliff reflected ruefully, remembering that the paternal sarcasms never lost any of their pungency by being well cogitated. That they were effervescing he could see by an occasional quiet smile in which his father indulged; but he was glad to have them kept in for the present.

"After I 've had another chance to try Sparkler," the boy said to himself, "then he may ask questions and have his joke."

Mr. Chantry was particularly fond of a joke at his children's expense. He never beat them, but his stinging ridicule was often worse than a whip.

"If Sparkler does n't sparkle next time, and I have to tell what I paid for him, won't I get it!" thought Cliff, watch-

ing the satirical quirk of the mouth in its parenthesis of
long, fine whiskers.

The afternoon waned, they finished their work, and the
subject uppermost in one mind, if not in both, was not
once mentioned. At the supper-table Susie and the
younger boys could talk of nothing but the dog in the
woodshed; and the mother scolded about it in her mild
way, alternately blaming Cliff for bringing the "creetur'"
home, and blaming the "creetur'" for ungratefully refusing to perform his tricks after he had been fed so bounti-
fully.

"He 's been asleep almost ever since you left him," said
Amos.   "I should n't think he 'd had any more sleep than
victuals lately.   He would n't even open his eyes for me."

"I told you not to go near him!" said Cliff, severely.

"I had to go there for an armful of wood," was the
younger brother's excuse.   "You 'll have to put him into
a bandbox, if he 's too precious to be looked at or spoken
to; or hang him in the well, as we do butter in hot weather, when we are out of ice."

The youngster's grin was a very good reduced copy of
the father's amused, ironic smile. The two were very
much alike, but for the paternal whiskers and a difference
of some thirty years in their ages.

After supper the cows were to be milked, and other
evening chores to be done; and all the while the dog was
left to his dreams and reflections in the darkening woodshed.   It was deep dusk when Quint Whistler strolled in
at the front gate, and Cliff went out to meet him.

"How's your ten-cent pup?" Quint inquired.

"He's humble, and I hope penitent," said Cliff. "Now, if we can have him alone, we'll see whether he can perform tricks, or whether we've dreamt it."

He let Quint into the woodshed, and went to the kitchen for a lamp. This he brought, followed by the younger boys, whom he cautioned to "keep quiet and hold their tongues" if they wanted to see the show.

"Now, Sparkler," he said, proceeding to remove the cord from the collar, "remember what you promised Mr. Winslow, and be a good dog. Treat me well, and I'll treat you well."

"I believe he understands," said Quint. "See how knowing he looks! I believe he's laughing!"

"We'll all laugh soon!" Cliff exclaimed hopefully, looking for a suitable stick in the pile of kindling-wood. "Shut that door, Susie!"

"Father says, bring the dog in," replied the girl, looking down from the kitchen doorway.

"Jehu! I can't do that!" Cliff muttered; "it'll spoil everything. Tell him I don't want to—just yet."

Susie disappeared, but returned with a peremptory message.

"He says, bring him in, whether you want to or not. If there's a show, he wants to see it."

"There won't be any show if I have him looking on and making fun," Cliff growled. "I suppose I shall have to, though. When he says a thing like that, he means it. You come too, Quint, and back me up. I know he won't do a thing!" And he threw down the stick in bitter discouragement.

To his surprise, Sparkler picked it up, and stood, with wagging tail, ready to follow him.

"See that! see that!" cried Amos and Trafton together. "He 's going to perform!"

"It looks more like it, sure!" said Cliff, thrilled with joyous expectation. "Out of the way, boys!" Then, to Susie: "Have all the doors shut, in there; for it 's a strange place, and there 's no knowing what he may do."

Preceded by the boys, and followed by Sparkler bearing the stick, Cliff entered the large, old-fashioned, lamp-lighted kitchen, Quint lagging awkwardly behind.

Mrs. Chantry at the same time came in from a room beyond, with a half-knitted stocking in her hand. The bright needles shone in the lamplight, and a dark thread of yarn meandered down across her white apron to a pocket, a bulge in which showed where the ball was lodged. Her kindly face was crinkled with smiles of anticipation as she saw Sparkler trotting along with the stick in his teeth.

Backed up toward a corner, under the clock, sat Mr. Chantry in a splint-bottomed rocker, parting his long, fleecy side-whiskers away from his shaven mouth and chin with the fingers of both hands, as his frequent habit was when preparing for a little pleasantry at the expense of the youngsters. Cliff, without looking at him, perceived the motion, and knew that his father's lips were twitching

and his eyes twinkling in a manner that boded mischief;
but he determined not to be disconcerted by him.

"Come along, Quint!" he cried, with an air of confidence. "Ame, give him a chair."

"I'm all right," said Quint, placing a flat stick across
a corner of the wood-box, and sitting on it.

With his hat removed, exposing a high, robust forehead,
he was a good-looking fellow, notwithstanding his disproportionate nose. He held his hat on his knee, and put an
arm around Trafton, the youngest boy, standing at his
side.

Cliff made his mother sit down, and placed a chair for
himself beside the table. There was a hush of suspense,
in which the old clock was heard ticking loudly, and the
farmer's chair squeaking as he rocked gently.

Cliff sat down, with the dog at his feet looking up inquiringly into his face.

"Sparkler," said he, "what are you going to do with
that stick?"

Immediately Sparkler got on his hind legs, holding up
the stick before his new master. The youngsters shrieked
with delight.

"I declare, if that ain't complete!" said the mother, staying her hands, which had begun to ply the knitting-needles
vigorously.

Mr. Chantry stopped rocking; he even stopped stroking
his whiskers.

Trembling with joy, yet almost afraid to ask anything
else of the dog, Cliff took the stick. Sparkler sat erect,

with his fore paws at his breast, and his bright, soft eyes wistfully studying his young master's face.

"Are you going to jump for me?" Cliff asked in a tone of affectionate comradeship.

The dog's whole body gave an eager start, his tail wagged, and one paw dropped.

"That means 'yes,'" Quint interpreted, from his seat on the wood-box.

Cliff could hardly keep from hugging the animal, so intense was his delight.

"Jump, then!" he said, holding out the stick. Sparkler leaped over it. "Higher!" he cried, suiting the action to the word. "Higher yet! Higher!" At each command, with its accompanying upward movement of the stick, the dog leaped to and fro with extraordinary liveliness, describing at each rebound a loftier curve.

"Did n't I tell you so?" said Cliff, triumphantly, with tears of pride and joy shining in his eyes. "He could jump over Ame's head; but I won't have him try, on this hard floor."

"Oh, yes; let him," said Amos. "I never had a dog jump over my head."

"Well, bring a rug for him to come down on," said Cliff.

But seeing that Sparkler was panting, Quint suggested that he should be allowed to rest a minute.

"Winslow," he said, "always let him rest between his tricks. He 's no slouch, is he, boys?"

Mrs. Chantry joined with the children in praising Sparkler's nimbleness and docility. Her husband forgot his whiskers, forgot his sarcasms, and leaned forward, with his arms on the arms of the chair, hardly less interested than the rest, although still wary of committing himself by any word of approval. The dog might yet make a failure, and give him an opportunity to get in some of his cutting remarks.

VII

CLIFF TRIUMPHANT

HE rug put in place, and Sparkler having recovered his breath, he made the leap over Ame's head in a manner that elicited applause from everybody but the non-committal farmer.

"Now, roll over!" said Cliff; which Sparkler promptly did, choosing the rug for his performance. Then Cliff cried, "Look alive!" and Sparkler was erect before him in a moment. "Give me a handkerchief, somebody."

Susie gave him hers, and he wrapped it around the end of the stick, which he set up between his feet.

"That's supposed to be a fire, and he's going to warm his hands. Warm your hands, Sparkler!"—which the dog did, sitting erect before the handkerchief, and holding up his paws before it with amusing mimicry.

"How's that for a ten-cent pup?" Quint asked in his dry way, as soon as the tumult of admiring exclamations had subsided.

"Ten cents!" exclaimed Mrs. Chantry. "You don't mean to say that 's what you paid!"

Cliff said nothing, but sat patting Sparkler's head, and breathing fast with excitement.

"That 's the price father guessed, and told Cliff he got cheated if he paid it," tittered Amos, while the father smiled and watched the dog.

"Now I 'll try his great trick, though I 'm by no means sure it will succeed," said Cliff. "How is it, Sparkler?" Sparkler sat up. "Will you do your best?"

He dropped one of his fore paws affirmatively, and the children cried out in jubilant chorus: "He will! He says he will!"

Then Cliff laid in a row on the floor, before the kitchen sink, the handkerchief, the stick, and one of the boys' hats, calling each article by name as he placed it.

"Now, father," he said, "which shall he fetch?"

Before Mr. Chantry could speak,—if, indeed, he was ready to take part in the exhibition he had expected to ridicule,—the boys clamored for the hat; and Mrs. Chantry said: "Yes, Cliff; I 'd like to see him fetch the hat."

Sparkler looked up inquiringly into Cliff's face.

"Fetch the hat," said Cliff; and the dog, obeying promptly, brought the hat and put it into his hands.

"It is past belief!" Mrs. Chantry exclaimed. "There 's witchery in it!"

"The witchery is all in his superior knowingness," said Cliff, proudly. "You 've no idea yet how bright he is. Fetch the stick, Sparkler!"

Sparkler brought the stick. Then Cliff replaced all the articles, and asked his father for a piece of money. Mr. Chantry hesitated, lifting his brows and looking quizzical, but finally put his hand in his pocket and produced a half-dollar. Cliff placed it under the hat.

"He 'll go straight for that, of course," said Amos.

"You 'll see," Cliff answered. "Ask for anything else."

So Amos named the handkerchief, which Sparkler brought, after waiting for his master to repeat the order. Then Cliff said: "Fetch the money from under the hat" —which the dog did, after experiencing some difficulty in getting the coin between his teeth.

Then Mr. Chantry for the first time opened his lips— not, however, to utter one of his premeditated sarcasms.

"How did you say you came by that dog?"

"A man by the name of Winslow sold him to me, this afternoon, down by Gibson's ice-house."

"I can't conceive of the owner of a dog like that wanting to sell him for any such price as a boy like you would be likely to give," said Mr. Chantry, gravely. "There must be some hidden reason back of it."

"Oh, he told us the reason," Cliff replied. "He was out of money, and he was on his way to his mother in Michigan. He was clerk in the big hotel in Bennington when it was burned two weeks ago. He lost everything by the fire, and that 's how he was obliged to part with the dog."

"Big hotel in Bennington?" queried the father.

"Yes; the Stark Hotel, was n't it, Quint?"

"Stark Hotel in Bennington!" pondered the farmer.

·"There may be a Stark Hotel there, for General Stark was a great man in that part of the country in Revolutionary times; he was in the battle of Bennington. But that's a small town, and I don't know what they wanted of a big hotel there."

"Maybe for summer boarders," Mrs. Chantry suggested.

"Possibly. But if any such great hotel has been burned lately, we should have seen something of it in the papers. And if he was on his way to Michigan, what brought him here?" Mr. Chantry argued. "This is out of his way."

"He did n't explain that," said Cliff. "Oh, I remember! He was going to stop in Buffalo, where he has friends."

"That does n't better the matter. I 'm afraid there 's some crookedness in the business. Ah!" Mr. Chantry had taken hold of the dog's collar, and was examining it. "No name, but here 's a place for one."

The strap was of maroon-colored leather, ornamented with a row of nickel studs set about an inch and a half apart. There were, however, two vacancies in this row—one where the collar buckled at the throat, the other where, instead of studs, there were two rivet-holes in the leather.

Mr. Chantry held the dog between his knees, Cliff and Quint kneeling to examine the collar with him, while Mrs. Chantry, stooping, held the lamp.

"I noticed those holes," said Quint; "and I supposed two of the studs had been lost out."

"It looks to me," said the farmer, "as if there had been a name-plate here, and as if it had been picked off—the rivets pried out of the leather. I'll wager something the fellow stole the dog."

"I can't think that!" exclaimed Cliff. "He was very particular to put it into the bargain that he was to have the privilege of buying him back. He made me give that to him in writing."

"And did he give you any writing?"

"Yes; a regular bill of sale."

"Let me see it."

The paper was produced. Mr. Chantry read the writing, pulled his left whisker, and mused:

"So you gave ten dollars in cash?" he said, lifting his eyes and looking straight at Cliff.

"Is n't he worth it?"

"I should say he was, and a good deal more. I don't at all approve of your buying him without my advice and consent; but 't was a temptation, and I sha'n't whale you for it." All the children laughed at what appeared to them as a good joke, Mr. Chantry (as we have hinted) not being in the habit of "whaling" his boys. "Did you have money enough to pay for him?"

"I still owe a little that I borrowed of Quint," Cliff answered.

"Pay it up," said his father, taking out his pocket-book.

But Cliff declined the proffered assistance.

"Quint is willing to wait," he said; "and I don't want anybody to have a claim on the dog except me—and Mr. Winslow. All I 'm afraid of now is that he 'll be coming with his twenty dollars to get him back."

"I guess you 'd better feed him a little now, had n't you?" said his mother. "He can have some bread and milk, as well as not."

"Let 's have some more tricks first," pleaded the youngsters.

"Well, just one or two, to please the children," she assented.

"Oh, ma!" Susie laughed, "you want to see the tricks just as much as we do. You know you do!"

Cliff was glad to put Sparkler again through some of his performances, which all remained to see, although it was bedtime for the boys. Then the dog was petted and fed, and taken back to the woodshed. Cliff gave him the rug to lie on, and patted him and talked to him as he slipped the cord once more through his collar, and made him fast to the frame of the grindstone.

"I sha'n't have to do this many times more," he said to his friend Quint, standing by; "but for a while it 's best to be on the safe side. Forgive me, Sparkler."

Taking affectionate leave of the dog, who licked his hand, he went out with Quint, and walked home with him; and they talked over the adventure under the stars, for half an hour longer, standing at Quint's gate.

"Well, good night, Quint!" he said at parting. "Has n't it been a great day? I owe ever so much to you!"

Then he returned home, to find his patient mother sitting up for him, after everybody else in the house had gone to bed. He took a last peep at his prize, curled up on the rug in the woodshed, saw that everything was quiet and

"MADE HIM FAST TO THE FRAME OF THE GRINDSTONE."

all doors fast, said "Good night" to his mother in a voice thrilling with happiness, received from her hand a candle she had lighted for him, and went up-stairs to bed. He was soon asleep, and dreaming of dogs that could swim in the air, balance poles on their noses, and play Brutus and Cassius for Mr. Algernon K. Winslow's edification.

VIII

ONE OF SPARKLER'S TRICKS

 HEN Cliff awoke in the morning, Spar-
kler was the first thing in his thoughts.
He hurriedly put on his clothes, and
hastened down-stairs, eager to learn
how his pet had passed the night, also
to assure himself that the wonderful
creature was a reality, and not a part of his vanished
dreams. He was astonished to meet Amos at the foot of
the chamber stairs. The boy was frightened, and hardly
able to speak.

"What's the matter?" Cliff demanded.

"Gone!" Amos whimpered.

"Who's gone? What's gone?"

"The dog."

"Not my trick-dog! Not Sparkler!" Cliff exclaimed in
wild consternation.

"Yes! skedaddled!" said Amos. "I was hurrying to
tell you."

"Who let him go?" Cliff asked fiercely, rushing past him.

"I did n't mean to," whined Amos. "I thought he was tied. I just opened the door to look at him, and he ran into the kitchen. That door was open, and he ran out."

"He *was* tied! Who untied him? Where is he?"

Cliff was already out of the house. At the corner of the woodshed he met his mother, pale with excitement.

"Which way did he go?" he demanded, hardly pausing for her reply as he ran past her.

"Down the road—toward the village," she answered, catching her breath. "He had a piece of the cord tied to his collar."

"A piece of it?" cried Cliff, turning back.

"Yes; just a few inches. I was standing by the stove when he went by me like a flash—in at one door, and out of the other, in an instant. I had just time to follow and get another glimpse of him before he was out of sight."

Cliff hurried to the woodshed to examine the cord. He found it tied to the grindstone, as he had left it; but Sparkler was off with the end fastened to his collar.

"He has gnawed it in two!" Cliff moaned.

Much the longer piece remained attached to the grindstone. With sudden resolution, he untied it, twisted it into a loose ball, and thrust it into his pocket.

"What are you going to do?" his mother asked, as he was hurrying from the woodshed.

"Follow him! Find him and bring him back!"

"Eat your breakfast first!" she entreated.

"I have n't a minute's time!" he declared.

4

"You may be away longer than you think. I 'll give you something to put into your pocket."

"Hurry up, then!"

He went with her into the kitchen, and came out presently with a piece of berry-pie in his hand, and his pockets bulging. He met his father approaching from the barn.

"What 's the trouble?" cried the farmer. "What 's the matter now?"

"My dog!" said Cliff. "He has gnawed off his cord and got away. Ame opened the door."

"Bah!" exclaimed his father. "That 's one of his tricks his owner did n't tell you of. You never 'll see him again."

"Yes, I will! He won't go farther than the Junction, where Winslow was to take the train; or, if he does, I can trace him."

"Let me go too!" Amos entreated. "I can leg it as fast as Cliff can."

"No, no!" said Mr. Chantry. "It 's bad enough to have one boy start off on such a wild-goose chase. You 'd better not go far, Cliff!" But Cliff was out of hearing, past the gate. "I would n't have had it happen for a good deal; I took quite a notion to that dog. Come, Amos; you must help about the chores."

"I let him out, and I ought to go and help find him," said Amos, making a merit of his share in the accident.

Just then the youngest son appeared, with hair uncombed, staring wildly, and highly incensed because he had been allowed to sleep at a time of such excitement.

"Any other morning I should have been called six times!" he complained. "Why did n't you ketch him by the tail, ma, when he shot by you?"

"I might as well have tried to ketch a streak of lightning by the tail," replied his mother. "I just heard a pattering sound, and he was out in a jiffy. He 's a mile away by this time, I warrant!"

IX

LIFF ran fast until he came in sight of Quint Whistler's home, on the outskirts of the village, and saw Quint himself standing in the open barn door. Quint's father, a mason and contractor, had just driven away to look after some business in an adjoining town, leaving Quint to shut up the barn and take care of the premises.

"Quint! Quint!" called Cliff, from the street. "My dog has got away!"

"Got away!" Quint called back, beginning to walk fast toward the gate. "Which way did he go?"

"Right past your place here; at least, he started this way. He'll most likely go straight to the shore, where he saw his master last, and then try to track him." Cliff stopped to gather breath, and added: "I'm so glad I've found you! Come along, won't you, and help me hunt him?"

"I don't know," said Quint, doubtfully. "As I was off

yesterday afternoon, I 'm expected to do some hoeing in the garden this morning.   That 's the order ! "

" So was I expected to work to-day," said Cliff, " but I can make it up ; and I 'll help you for all the time you lose. We may overhaul him in an hour."

" And it may take all day !   Besides, I have n't had my breakfast," Quint objected.

" Neither have I !   Take a bite in your hand, and something in your pockets, as I have."

As he spoke Cliff seemed to remember the wedge of pie he carried, which he had n't yet thought of eating.   He took a deep mouthful, staining his lips with the juice of the berries with which it was filled ; while Quint, as deliberate in thought and action as his friend was impetuous, balanced considerations.

" Of course I must help you out of this," he said at length.   " I 'll be with you in a minute."

He entered the house, and presently came out, stuffing his pockets with doughnuts.

" Whether it 's to be a long or a short chase," he said, " you can count me in.   I helped you buy him, and I 'll stick by you as long as there 's a chance of running him down."

And the chase began.

They learned by inquiries that Sparkler had kept on straight to the village, and had been seen taking the railroad-track where it crossed the main street.

" He has found the shortest cut to the shore," said Cliff, surprised at this new evidence of the animal's sagacity—

the boys having conducted him by the more circuitous way of the streets, the day before.

There was a well-trodden foot-path along the edge of the railroad embankment; this they took, without pausing to look for dog-tracks, and soon reached the spot where Cliff had made his purchase.

It was a fine summer morning. A gentle southwest wind was blowing cool across the lake; the sunshine glittered on the rippling water, and gilded the long grass and low willows that waved by the shore. But to give interest to the scene, in the eyes of Quint and Cliff, one small animate thing was needful—a dog that would have been to them, just then, the most delightful object within the ring of the horizon. But no dog was anywhere in sight.

Two men were loading ice into a wagon backed up against the ice-house. Cliff called out to them.

"Yes," one called back, in reply to his inquiries; "we saw a dog come down to the pond just a little while ago. He snuffed around awhile, and capered up and down, then started off down the railroad-track as fast as he could clip it."

"He seemed to have a little piece of rope, or something, dangling from his neck," said the other man.

"That's my dog! He's gone straight to the Junction! We'll overhaul him there!" Cliff said confidently to his companion, as they hurried on.

It was nearly a mile to the Junction. They kept the railroad-track all the way, but saw nothing of the fugitive.

On the platform they found the station-master checking a trunk, and Cliff accosted him breathlessly.

"No," he said; "I have n't noticed any such dog."

"That is strange," said Cliff. "Did you sell a ticket, yesterday afternoon at about four o'clock, to a young man —had on a narrow-brimmed hat, kind of a checkered straw?"

"Stand-up collar, a little stained about the edges," added Quint. "Small mustache—tip looked at a little distance as if it had been streaked with charcoal."

The station-master remembered him very well; he had sold him a ticket, and noticed that he had no baggage, not even a gripsack, when he stepped aboard the train.

"That 's all right!" cried Cliff. "That man sold me a dog yesterday. He was a trick-dog, and he got away this morning. We were afraid, if the man did n't take the train, but kept afoot, the dog might track him. It looks as if he was honest!"

"It looks more so than it did. But where 's the dog?" said Quint.

The station-master called to a switch-tender, who approached, and said, in answer to Cliff's questions:

"Yes; I saw that very dog half or three quarters of an hour ago. I noticed the bit of rope hanging from his collar. He snuffed about the platform, and run in and out of the waiting-room; then all of a sudden he seemed to remember a previous engagement, and put out toward Tressel, with a full head of steam on."

"Did he take the track?" Cliff asked.

"No; the street."

Tressel was a station a mile or more beyond, which could be reached by either highway or rail.

"Come on," cried Cliff, eagerly. "He's going the wrong direction to find Winslow. He'll fetch up somewhere."

But Quint was deliberating.

"Wait a minute! I want to be sure of a thing or two. You say that man bought a ticket. Was it to go West?"

"No," said the station-master; "he bought a ticket for Kilbird."

Kilbird being the first station beyond Tressel, Cliff was astonished.

"He said he was going West!"

"No matter what he said; he took the east-bound accommodation train, sure!" said the station-master, positively. He was beginning to show a kindly interest in the two boys and their adventure.

It took Cliff a moment to recover from his bewilderment; then he turned to Quint, and said:

"I'd like your company ever so much, and I don't know what I shall do without you—you think of more things than I do, and look further ahead. But I'm afraid this is going to be a long pull, and I know I ought not to drag you along."

"If you call it dragging, why, I'll turn back," said Quint. "I know I'm slow."

"I don't mean that!" cried Cliff. "But I've no right to ask so much of you; that's what I meant to say."

"Then don't say it again!" Quint replied, starting off resolutely on the road to Tressel and Kilbird. "Come on!"

X

THE BEGINNING OF THE CHASE

HE boys now settled down to a fast walk, munching crackers and doughnuts by the way, and discussing, between bites, Sparkler's chance of rejoining his late master. That such was the dog's instinctive object, both agreed; but they were not yet quite sure of the part Mr. Algernon Winslow was playing.

They got news of the fugitive by the way, and, on reaching Tressel, met three boys, who gave them some interesting information. They had seen the dog with the dangling piece of cord pass through the village in the direction of Kilbird; and one of them reported having seen, the day before, a man offering to sell just such a dog to a teamster watering his horses at the wayside trough.

Cliff inquired: "Did you notice which way the man with the dog came from?"

"He came from the direction of Kilbird," said the boy, "and he went on toward Biddicut Junction."

Quint thought a moment, then observed:

"It's all as plain to me as this doughnut. Winslow came from Kilbird, or some place around there, yesterday; he took the train to Kilbird after selling you the dog; and now the dog has gone back there to meet him. See?"

Cliff did see, greatly to his chagrin and vexation. Just then a locomotive whistled.

"Here comes the down train!" he exclaimed. "How would it do for one of us to board it for Kilbird, and try heading him off that way, while the other keeps the road?"

"That's judgmatical," said Quint. "We've just time to buy a ticket. Have you got any money?"

"Jehu! I forgot all about money!" cried Cliff. "I gave the last of mine to you, yesterday."

"And I put it away in my box after I got home," replied Quint. "It never occurred to me to take any for this trip."

"Of course it did n't!" Cliff declared. "It was n't your business to; it belonged to me to provide for expenses. It's just like me! I should have come off without any breakfast if my mother had n't made me take something. She did n't think of money, for I suppose she never expected I would go far."

So that scheme had to be given up.

"Never mind," said Quint, consolingly. "The dog will be in Kilbird before the train will, if he is n't there already. It will be better for us to keep together."

"Yes. But see here, Quint! This is growing serious, and there's no use of my getting you any deeper into the scrape. Now, you *must* go back."

"That 's a friendly way of looking at it," Quint replied; "but I 'm going to see the fun out, now I 've started."

The train had come and gone, and was already passing out of sight. The boys followed, keeping the highway. The dangling cord was a fortunate circumstance, for it attracted attention to the runaway, and rendered the pursuit comparatively easy.

They had been walking some time on a lonely country road, without meeting any one of whom they could make inquiries, when Cliff said:

"There comes a team; we 'll ask the driver."

"Is it a team?" Quint replied in a dry, argumentative tone which caused Cliff to turn and look at him; for when Quint spoke in that way his friends generally knew that something quizzical was coming.

"It looks like it," said Cliff — "a horse and wagon and a driver."

"Which is the team?" Quint asked. "The driver?"

"Not exactly."

"The horse?"

"Well, yes, the horse—partly, at least."

"You sometimes hear folks talk of getting into a team," Quint went on. "They don't mean getting into the horse, do they?"

"They mean the wagon, of course," Cliff said. "I never thought of it before, but it seems a trifle mixed."

"It 's a good deal mixed," Quint replied. "Now, you 'll be surprised to learn that the wagon is no more a part of the team than the driver is, and that one horse does n't make a team any more than one blade makes scissors. A team, according to the dictionary, is two or more animals harnessed or yoked together for drawing—something like that."

"Jehu!" Cliff ejaculated; "how did you ever get to know so much?"

"Oh, sister Jenny!"

Quint's sister Jenny was a school-teacher, whose erudition in some particulars he often found more useful in puzzling his friends than in correcting his own frequent faults of language.

"So you see, Cliff, your team is no team, and when people speak—"

He stopped suddenly, and stood staring straight before him down the turnpike.

"By hokey, Cliff!" he exclaimed, "I know that team!"

"No, you don't, Quint!" Cliff replied.

"Why do you say I don't, when I say I do, and can prove it?" Quint demanded.

"Because I can prove that you don't," Cliff answered. "You can't see a thing where no such thing is, can you? And can you know a team when, according to your own showing, there is no team? Ask Jenny!"

"You owed me one, and you 've paid it, as our friend Winslow said yesterday," Quint replied, laughing. "Anyhow, I know the horse, for I harnessed him this morning. The wagon is our carryall, and the driver is my father."

"There is n't any doubt about that," said Cliff. "Oh,

Quint! if we could only borrow the—what do ye call it? team or no team—horse and wagon!"

"I 'd like to have you ask him!" Quint chuckled.

Mr. Whistler was much surprised, on drawing near, to meet his own boy and a neighbor's traveling that dusty road so far from home. He listened with amused interest to Quint's story of the runaway dog.

"Did he bite you both, and give you the running-away distemper?" he asked. "I have n't seen him, and I don't believe you can catch him any more than you could catch a fox on Wachusett Mountain! Get into the wagon here, and ride back with me, both of you; that 's the wisest thing you can do."

"Quint can; I guess it 's the wisest thing for him," said Cliff. "But I shall keep on till I find the dog or drop down in my tracks."

"Get up here, Quint; no more nonsense!" the elder Whistler commanded. "Cliff can do as he likes."

"He would like to borrow a little money of you, anyway," said Quint. "We have both come away without any."

Mr. Whistler demurred. "I don't know what his father 'll say to my lending him money for such a tomfool expedition."

"My father knows what I am doing, and he 'll be obliged to you for giving me a little help," Cliff put in.

"Well, about how much do you want?" said the mason and contractor, putting his hand in his pocket.

"Enough to take me home from Kilbird by the train, anyway," said Cliff, "and maybe a trifle over."

"Enough to take us both home," Quint added —"if I go with him."

"It 's a foolish business," Mr. Whistler commented; "but if Cliff's father approves, I don't know why I should stand out"—leaning over the wagon-side as he reached down a handful of small change. "Will this do?"

"Oh, yes! Ever so much obliged!" cried Cliff, delightedly, pocketing the money. "If you see any of my folks, please tell 'em—"

"I 'll tell 'em I saw you going off in company with another lunatic," said the elder Whistler, driving on.

XI

ANOTHER DOG-HUNTER

THE boys laughed as they resumed their tramp.

"These fathers," observed Cliff, "have some good points, after all!"

"We have to take 'em as they come; we can't pick and choose our own," Quint replied. "Mine is like yours in one way: his bark is worse than his bite. When I propose a thing, he'll almost always say, 'No; silly notion!' But if I give him line,—play with him as you would with a trout too heavy for your tackle,—I can generally wind him in. 'Yes, yes; do go along!'—just what I wanted him to say in the first place. But if I insist too hard, it's no use; he's like one of his own stone walls—built to stand."

"A boy of any gumption soon finds out how to manage his parents," said Cliff. "My mother likes to scold, and I just let her; it does n't hurt a bit! It's a good pie that sputters in the oven; did you ever notice it? She's just awfully nice, after she gets over it. But my father's tongue is the worst; he is so sarcastic!"

69

So they went on, discussing the home-rule question in a manner that would have edified their respective fathers and mothers.

"But mine, both of 'em," said Cliff, "would do anything for their children; and I should be about the meanest boy in the world to say anything against them!" he added, with a quaver of emotion in his voice.

"I tell you what, Cliff," Quint replied. "If ever it comes our turn to be talked over as we are talking over our folks now, I only hope our boys won't have any more cause to find fault than we have; that 's all!"

Meanwhile they kept up their inquiries for Sparkler. Nobody on that part of the highway had seen a dog with a cord dangling from his collar, nor, indeed, any stray dog.

"He may have turned off on some other road, or taken to the fields," said Cliff, at length. "What shall we do?"

"I believe our best way is to keep straight on to Kilbird," said Quint. "If we don't strike his trail there, we may at least hear from Winslow."

"There comes another 'team'!" laughed Cliff.

The "team" in this instance was a man on horseback. The horse was a heavy, hard-trotting animal, and the rider a stout little man, who at every jolt went up and down like a bouncing ball. Neither horse nor rider seemed accustomed to the saddle; indeed, there was no saddle between them—only a blanket, bound in place by a surcingle. Over this curved the little man's legs, unsupported by stirrups.

He was approaching along a by-road, and the boys stopped on a corner to speak with him. At the same time he kicked the horse's sides and struck him with the reins, appearing even more anxious for an interview than they were.

Before they could accost him, he called out, with the jolts in his voice, as the animal's ponderous trot broke to a walk:

"Say—have—you—seen—a—stray—dog—along—here—anywheres?"

It seemed almost as if he must have known their business, and that he was a joker, who took this means of heading off their expected inquiries. But there was no sign of facetiousness in that round russet face.

Quint gave Cliff a nudge, and said, with a droll twist of his mouth:

"Seems to be a pretty good day for stray dogs!"

"What sort of a dog?" Cliff asked.

"A ruther small dog," said the man. "Kind of curly brown hair. A sort of spaniel. Had on a collar fastened with a buckle; sort of reddish-brown luther, with bright studs in it."

The boys listened with astonishment, the description fitted Sparkler so exactly. Only the dangling piece of cord was lacking.

"What do you want of that dog?" Cliff demanded.

"Naterally," said the man, "I want to find him and fetch him home."

"Does he belong to you?"

5

"He 'd oughter belong to me, for I bought him and paid for him."

"When was that?"

"Day before yis'day. A man brought him along and offered him for sale. He showed how well he would watch a coat, and I got him for a watch-dog. Give a five-dollar bill for him! He wanted twenty-five, but I beat him down to five. My name is Miller; I live over in Wormwood."

Cliff's throat had become so dry that he could n't utter another word. Quint took up the colloquy.

"How did he get away from you?"

Mr. Miller eased his position by leaning sidewise on his horse, and explained:

"The man advised me to keep him shet up for a day or two, and I put him into the barn. I fed him well, and he seemed as contented as if I 'd always owned him. A couple of hours later I went to look at him. It was kind o' dusky in the barn; I could n't see him nowheres; so I spoke to him, and opened the door jest a crack wider— swish! he zipped past my legs out o' that door like a kicked foot-ball! That 's the last I 've seen of him."

"Did n't you try to follow him?" Quint inquired.

"Yes; but 't was so near night, 't wa'n't no use. Yis'-day I had an all day's job o' teaming, and I said: 'The dog 's got his supper, and the man 's got his five dollars, and hang 'em! let 'em go!' But half an hour ago a neighbor come over to say he 'd seen that dog, this morn-ing, over by the Lippitt place, this side of Tressel. He tried to head him off, but he took to the woods, and he lost sight of him. So I jest throws a blanket on old Bob, and jogs off to hunt him up. You hain't seen no such animal?" Mr. Miller continued, talking down to the boys.

"Not to-day," Quint replied; "but I saw that very dog yesterday afternoon. A man offered him for sale, over in Biddicut, and a neighbor of mine bought him for ten dollars. He got cheated worse than you did!"

Mr. Miller straightened himself excitedly, and tightened his loose bridle-reins, eager to resume his hard trot.

"Yes, he did," he cried, "for he bought my dog! Where is he?"

"The boy or the dog?" Quint inquired.

"Both!" said Mr. Miller.

"The boy is right here before you," said Quint, laying his hand on Cliff's shoulder. "But where the dog is, we're as anxious to know as you are. He got away this morning, and we tracked him a good piece this side of Tressel village—to about where your neighbor saw him, I should say. His taking to the woods accounts for our losing all trace of him."

Mr. Miller was starting off, but he pulled rein to say:

"I was afraid the man was a rogue! But he told a straight story about bein' a clerk in a hotel that was burned, up in Brattleboro."

"Brattleboro?" cried Cliff. "He told us Bennington!"

"Brattleboro!" Mr. Miller insisted positively. "And he was going to the bedside of a sick mother in Wisconsin."

"Michigan! He told us Michigan!" Cliff exclaimed.
"Did n't he?" appealing to Quint.

Mr. Miller gave him a parting look of disgust, then
kicked his clumsy heels into the horse's ribs, slapped him
with the looped end of the reins, clucked like a hen and
threw up his arms like wings, and started off on his hard-
trotting beast.

The boys watched his bouncing ball of a body for a
moment with mingled emotions, then turned and looked
at each other.

"Well, Cliff!" Quint said, with a strange smile.

Cliff was so astounded by the proof of Winslow's bad
faith that he made two or three attempts to speak before
he finally replied:

"Quint, it 's no use! We may as well turn around and
go home."

"How do you work that out?" Quint inquired.

"Don't you see? I 've no claim on that dog, anyway!
If Winslow had a right to sell him, he belongs to Miller,
who bought him before I did."

"I can't help laughing!" Quint suddenly broke forth.
"It 's awfully funny, come to think of it! Algernon K.
Winslow is a man of genius; he has invented a new business—selling a dog! Who knows how many times he
had sold him before he sold him to Miller? Your title is
probably as good as Miller's."

"It may be, and yet not be worth taking this tramp
for," Cliff answered despondently.

"I beg to differ with you. Possession, they say, is nine

points of the law. If we get possession of that dog,"
Quint continued, "we can hold him till somebody shows
a better claim; and if the rightful owner turns up, I 'm
sure he 'll be willing to pay your ten-dollar mortgage on
him, and other expenses. There 's no discount on that
dog, Cliff; the discount is all on Winslow."

Cliff's face brightened. "There 's a good deal in what
you say, Quint!"

"It 's judgmatical!" said Quint.

He gave a last look at the disappearing horseman, and
said smilingly:

"Mr. Miller is welcome to all the satisfaction he will
get from his trip to the Lippitt place. We 'll hunt for
both man and dog at Kilbird; and it 's my humble opinion that the man will be about as well worth catching as
the dog. I 'll squeeze your ten dollars out of him!" he
concluded, clenching his fist, while his strong features
settled into an expression of grim resolution.

XII

THE VILLAGE LANDLADY

HE boys had already resumed their tramp. Cliff no longer thought of going back.

At Kilbird they turned the corner of a cross-street in order to reach the railroad-station, which lay in a little valley between two divisions of the village. They put their usual question to a boy standing on the front steps of a grocer's store.

He had seen no such dog that morning. "But," said he, "there was a man here yesterday with one, trying to sell him."

In answer to Cliff's inquiries, he described Winslow and Sparkler very accurately, and added:

"They came from over the railroad, and I heard somebody say the man was stopping at the Grover House."

"The Grover House?" cried Cliff, eagerly. "Where is that?"

"It 's the hotel you see on the rise of ground the other side of the railroad—the house with the porch and balcony, and the balm-o'-Gilead trees in front."

Uttering hasty thanks for this information, the two dog-hunters hurried down the near slope and up the farther one without halting at the station, and called up at a woman they saw shaking a rug on the balcony behind the balm-of-Gilead trees. She answered, looking down over the rail, that she did n't know any guest of the house named Winslow.

"A man with a dog," Cliff shouted back, adding a few words of description.

"I know who you mean," she replied. "He has been here, off and on, for a couple of days, and he may be here yet; he was, an hour or two ago. I 'll speak to Mrs. Grover."

Mrs. Grover proved to be the landlady, who presently came out on the porch beneath the balcony to speak to the boys.

"Why, yes," she said, "Mr. Knight—a very nice man! And the wonderfullest dog I ever did see! He spent the night here, last night, and the night before. He has n't been gone much more than half an hour."

"Gone?" Cliff gasped out, standing with one foot on the porch step. "And the dog—did he have the dog?"

"I 'll tell you about that," replied the landlady. "He lost the dog, someway, yesterday, and came back last evening without him. The dog did n't come till this morning. Mr. Knight seemed to be waiting for him. He said the dog had a bad trick of straying off, but that he always turned up again."

Cliff stepped up on the porch floor, and said earnestly:

"The man you call Mr. Knight told me his name was Algernon Knight Winslow; and he sold me that dog yesterday for ten dollars."

The landlady of the Grover House expressed a great deal of surprise and sympathy, and invited the boys to sit down and rest on a bench in the cool porch.

"You look kind of beat out," she said, noticing that they were flushed and covered with dust.

But Cliff said they were not tired; they could n't stop —they were bound to follow Winslow; and he asked:

"Did he take a train?"

"No; he hired my husband to drive him over to Corliss in his buggy. It 's only about three miles, and Mr. Grover will be back now very soon. I 'm awfully sorry for your bad luck!" said the good woman. "I would n't have believed Mr. Knight was such a man. My husband called him a smooth-tongued fellow, and he did n't take much stock in his stories; but he never suspected him of dishonesty."

Quint inquired: "Did he have any baggage?"

"Only a small linen bag, which he left here when he was off on excursions. But he took it with him this morning, saying he did n't expect to come back. I must do him the justice to say he paid his bill."

"Well he might, with other people's money!" Cliff exclaimed. "How many times did his dog stray away?"

"Twice anyway," replied Mrs. Grover. "Mr. Knight came home without him day before yesterday; but the dog came the same evening."

"That's the time he sold him to Miller," said Cliff, turning to his companion. "I wonder how many times more he has sold him?"

"More times than he ever will again, if we lay hands on either of 'em!" laughed Quint.

Mrs. Grover became exceedingly friendly and sympathetic, and insisted on opening a bottle of spruce-beer for the wayfarers while they rested on the shaded bench. It was a welcome refreshment, which Cliff offered to pay for, but she laughingly told him to "put up his money." Then, perceiving that they nibbled furtively at something they brought out from their pockets between sips, she entered the house, and presently reappeared with two generous sandwiches, consisting of slices of excellent buttered bread, lined with cold sliced ham.

"This is too much!" Cliff exclaimed, with glistening eyes.

"You seem to be proper nice boys," she replied, "and I'm only too glad to give you a little treat after you have been so imposed upon. I shall want you to write your names in our book. I'll bring it out here, with a pen, so you can be resting all the while."

"Cliff," said Quint, glancing over his shoulder to see that she was out of hearing (he held his glass in one hand and his bitten sandwich in the other), "if I was n't already fitted out with a tolerably good mother, I know where I'd go to adopt one!"

Cliff nodded and winked, and whispered, as he lifted his glass to his lips: "She's coming back."

She brought the hotel register, and, laying it open on Cliff's knees, offered him a freshly dipped pen. Cliff set his glass down beside him, laid his half-eaten sandwich across the top of it, took the pen, and passed it to Quint.

"You write first," he said.

"No; you write for both," said Quint. "You were always the champion ink-slinger of our class."

"When you say that, I can't write at all," Cliff laughed; "I 'm afraid of my own reputation. I 'll try my skill at your name first; it won't matter if I do spoil that."

"You can't make it any homelier than I am," replied Quint. "Put in the gambrel-roof nose!" As Mrs. Grover glanced at his prominent feature, and smiled, he added: "That 's none of my wit; it 's Winslow's. He gave my nose that label before a dozen boys, and it 's going to stick. We got so much out of him."

Cliff wrote, in a fair round hand, "J. Q. A. Whistler," saying as he raised the pen:

"That small regiment of initials stands for 'John Quincy Adams.' I was afraid there would n't be ink enough to write out the name in full, and I did n't want to keep you running to the inkstand."

Then Cliff wrote his own name, "Clifford P. Chantry," made a loop against both names, and at the right of it put the address, "Biddicut."

"I declare," exclaimed Mrs. Grover, looking down from over the end of the bench, "I know your mother! She was Lucinda Clifford, and she married Jonathan Chantry!

"'HERE'S OUR FRIEND'S NAME, CLIFF!'"

We were school-girls together, and I was at her wedding. We used to exchange visits, but it's an age now since we've seen each other. Tell her you've made the acquaintance of Emmeline Small that was, now Mrs. Robert Grover, and that my husband keeps the Grover House, here in Kilbird."

"She'll be pleased enough," said Cliff; "and when I tell her how you treated two strange boys, it is n't going to make her sorry she ever knew you. She'll come and visit you some time, I promise you."

"I shall be glad to see her, or any of your folks," said the cordial landlady.

She offered to remove the hotel book, but Quint asked to look at it.

"Just a second," he said. "Here's our friend's name, Cliff! did you notice it? A little twisted,—'A. W. Knight,'—with a flourish as long as the cord he gave you to lead the dog by!"

"Burlington!" Cliff exclaimed, reading the address. "He told us 'Bennington'; he told Mr. Miller 'Brattleboro'; and here he is,"—slapping the register,—"Burlington, Vermont!"

"The trouble with that man is, he forgets," said Quint. "He forgets his own name, and he forgets all but the first letter of the name of the place he did n't come from. He gets the B right every time—writes it large, as if it was a bumble-B; but he can't remember the whole word, any more than he can the fact that he has sold his dog when he gets a chance to sell him over again. He'll forget us,

Cliff, if we don't hurry along and overhaul him. We'll refresh his memory!"

He stepped to the edge of the porch, and brushed the crumbs from his clothes, then, turning to Cliff and the landlady, remarked in his driest tones:

"If Winslow had been true to his name, and had n't tried to win so fast, 't would have been better for all concerned."

XIII

MRS. GROVER'S HUSBAND

HE boys were rested and refreshed, and impatient to be off. The landlady urged them to remain, saying that she expected her husband's return at any moment, that he would bring news of Winslow's movements, and that she would make him "give them a lift in his team."

"Why not start on and meet him?" said Cliff. "It will save time."

"That's judgmatical," said Quint; and Mrs. Grover admitted that it was probably their best plan.

She described her husband's "team," which turned out to be a white-nosed horse and an open buggy, at which the boys smiled, remembering their previous discussion.

"And tell him," she called after them from the porch, "that I said he was to wheel about and carry you a piece on the Corliss road. He can do it as well as not!"—raising her voice as, having thanked her, they were hurrying away. "Tell him I said so!"

"There are some pretty decent folks in this world, with all the rogues," was Quint's quiet observation, as they put on their hats, after waving them in farewell, while the landlady stood smilingly watching their departure.

"It 's worth all the trouble that scamp Knight Winslow is giving us, just to have fallen in with such a woman as Mrs. Grover—'Emmeline Small that was,'" said Cliff, who could n't help indulging in a little gentle pleasantry, even at the expense of so kind a woman. "I never tasted such spruce-beer, did you?"

"And such sandwiches!" Quint exclaimed. "Fact is, we were in just the right shape for spruce-beer and ham sandwiches to hit us in a tender spot, with a little womanly kindness thrown in."

"If Mrs. Grover's husband will be half as kind to a couple of 'proper nice boys,'" laughed Cliff, "and give us that ride in his 'team'—say, there he is now!"

"It 's the white-nosed horse and open buggy, anyhow," said Quint. "But it is n't quite my idea of Mr. Grover," he added, as the driver drew near.

"Nor mine, by Jehu!" cried Cliff.

They had pictured to themselves a bright, alert, good-looking man, a worthy mate of the woman who had won their hearts. The driver of the white-nosed horse had a listless air and a weak face, "about as bright-looking" (Quint muttered) "as a rusty plowshare." He was driving slowly, with slack reins, and seemed to be regarding his horse's heels so intently that he gave no heed to the boys until they hailed him from the roadside.

"Is this Mr. Grover?" cried Cliff.

"Whoa! That's my name when I'm to home," said Mrs. Grover's husband.

"You have just carried Mr. Win—Mr. Knight over to Corliss," said Cliff.

"Yes, and a little beyend," said Mrs. Grover's husband. Then, as the boys questioned him : "I set him down at the first mile-stone on the Popham turnpike. You want him?"

"Yes; we want him bad!" said Cliff. "He has got my dog!"

"*Your* dog?" queried the landlord of the Grover House.

"He sold him to me yesterday," replied Cliff; "but he gnawed his rope and got away."

"That accounts for it—the piece that was hanging from his collar when he came back to the hotel this morning," said Mr. Grover.

"Such cord as this?" cried Cliff, pulling a coil from his pocket.

"Exactly! Knight pretended somebody had tried to steal him. It's curious, about that dog! I thought there might be something wrong when I noticed the way the name had been taken off the collar."

"Was there a name?" cried Cliff. "He told us they did n't have to put names and numbers on dogs' collars up in Vermont."

"He told *me* the plate with his name on it had been stolen by some thief who must have thought it was silver," replied the landlord. "I said I should have thought it

would be easier to steal collar and all than to pull out the
rivets and leave the collar; and he said, 'It would seem
so.' He wanted to sell *me* the dog. He made him ride in
the buggy with us this morning, so as to keep him fresh,
I suppose, for trying his trick over again. You did n't lay
eyes on a horseshoe anywhere on the road, as you came
along, did you?"

"No, we did n't; we had something else to think of,"
said Cliff.

"My nag has cast one, somewhere, since I left home,"
said Mr. Grover; "but I did n't notice it till he began to
favor that off hind foot. I 've been looking for it all the
way back. Hope you 'll have better luck finding your
man. He 's got considerable the start of you, but he was
walking kind o' leisurely—leastwise, he was when I last
saw him; and he 'll be known by a flat linen bag he car-
ries, as well as by the dog."

He was starting on, when Quint nudged his companion,
muttering:

"Why don't you ask him?"

"I hoped he would offer," Cliff replied. "I hate to
beg!"

"It won't be begging, since his wife told you. Hello,
Mr. Grover!" Quint called after the departing "team."

It stopped, and Cliff, feeling that it was his affair, and
not Quint's, stepped quickly to the side of the buggy.

"Mrs. Grover was very good to us when we stopped at
the house, and she said you would carry us a piece on the
road to Corliss."

"She did ?" said the landlord, looking down kindly but curiously at the honest-faced boy. "Just like her, for all the world ! "

Cliff hastened to add : "Of course I shall expect to pay you."

"'T ain't that ; it 's the horseshoe I 'm considering," said Mr. Grover. "I could n't drive fast without laming that off hind leg ; and if I was to drive slow, you might as well foot it. Sorry, but you see how it is."

Cliff had regarded the lost horseshoe as a very trivial affair ; but he found it was a matter of importance, even to him. He could n't help showing his disappointment, but he answered cheerily : "I should n't want to injure your horse. Just as much obliged ! "

And he said to Quint, as they hurried away :

"Now we must make up for lost time ! It 's lucky we did n't wait for him at the Grover House."

"I don't know about that," replied Quint. "If Mrs. Grover is the woman I take her to be, she 'd have made him harness another horse—unless it 's a one-horse hotel. Maybe she 'll send him after us. She 's the captain of that company of two. Grover 's the rank and file ! "

Fortunately the boys made no delay in expectation of a fresh horse being sent after them, but walked fast, feeling that success in their pursuit depended on their own strong limbs and resolute wills.

6

XIV

"A NICE PET FOR AN OLD COUPLE"

T took them a full half-hour to reach the mile-stone on the Popham turnpike where Mr. Grover had set down Winslow and his dog.

They found the spot where the buggy-wheels had turned, leaving their semi-circles in the dust of the road. Yes, and there were fresh footprints of a dog—Sparkler's, beyond question. They looked in vain for Winslow's, and concluded that he must have alighted on one of the grassy borders. The dog's, moreover, were soon lost, or could be seen again so rarely beyond the mile-stone that the boys quickly decided to waste no precious moments in looking for them, but to press on, as they had done earlier in the morning, in the direction the dog and his master must have taken.

Farm-houses were few, and they met no vehicles, and nobody had any information to give until they came to some mowers whetting their scythes in a field beside the road. Cliff leaned over the wall and put his usual question.

"Yes; and he wanted to sell his dog to us," one of the men answered back, poising his whetstone and feeling the edge of his scythe. "About an hour ago. But he found this a poor dog-market."

"Which way did he go?"

"Straight ahead."

Whacky-te-whack! went the whetstones on the bright blades, to the music of which the boys hastened on. They received further and equally positive information from time to time, and at length, high in hope, entered a small village to which they had traced the fugitives.

It was a village of scattered houses, in front of one of which they found a bareheaded man leaning over a gate. His back was toward them, and he seemed to be gazing very intently up the street. Farther on were other people in doorways or front yards, or standing in the street, all gazing in the same direction.

By his leather apron and the sign over his door, the boys perceived that the man leaning on the gate was a shoemaker.

"What's the show?" Quint asked.

"Show!" said the man, turning upon him a look of disgust. "There ain't no show! And I'm fooled out of five dollars—clean as a whistle!"

Cliff asked how that had come about, and the man told his story to an intensely interested audience of two.

"A man come along here about an hour ago, and stopped into my shop to git me to rasp a nail out of his boot. He had a dog he bragged about, and made him do some tricks that I thought my woman would like to see. We hain't got no childern, and last winter a neighbor's dog killed our cat—got holt of her in the deep snow, where she had no chance; she could gener'ly scratch up a tree or take care of herself, anyway, but this time the poor thing got left. We missed her, and had been wishin' for some kind of a pet; and when my wife heard the man say he had got out of money and would have to part with his dog, she looked at me, and I nodded, and then she says, 'How much do you ask for him?' she says. When he said, 'Twenty dollars,' I thought, of course, 't wa'n't no use for us to think of buyin' him; but as he wanted me to make him an offer, I looked at my wife, and she nodded to me, and I says, 'I 'll give three,' I says, without the least idee he 'd take me up. He did n't exactly, but he come down to ten dollars, then to seven, then said he 'd split the difference; and I looked at my wife, and she winked to me, and I says, 'All right,' I says; 'I 'll give ye five'—though I wish to gracious now I 'd stuck to my first bid."

"You bought him for five dollars?" cried Cliff.

"Yes, on condition that the man should have the privilege of buyin' him back for double the money, any time within a month. He 's jest the cutest dog you ever set eyes on; he seemed such a nice pet for an old couple! And after the man was gone, my wife she says, 'I do hope he never 'll come back for him!' and I said I hoped so, too."

"Where 's the dog now?" Cliff asked, although he knew well enough already.

The man threw his thumb over his shoulder in the direction in which he and the other villagers had been gazing.

"Skipped!" he said. "Skipped like a flea! We 'd fed him in the shop, with the doors closed; and he was so nice and quiet, my wife wanted to have him a little while in the kitchen; and I said, 'Yes; only keep him shet in for the present,' I said, for the owner advised us to do that till he 'd had time to get well out of the way. There 's only a door 'twixt shop and kitchen, and I was hammerin' away at a strip of so'-luther when I heard her scream, and she come rushin' in to say the dog was gone."

"Did n't you have him tied?" Quint inquired.

"I jest had a strap buckled to his collar at first; but he seemed so contented, I took it off to let him run around indoors. There was jest a winder open, over the kitchen sink; but we did n't think nothin' about that, and he did n't seem to, nuther, till all to once—whish! he was up on that sink, and out o' that winder, 'fore the scream was out of her mouth. I 've got the rheumatiz, and can't run; but she rushed out. There she comes now!"

"Without the dog!" said Cliff, gazing eagerly.

The shoemaker's wife had to run the gantlet of questions from all her neighbors, as she returned, with excited looks and panting breath, to her husband.

"I never see the beat on 't!" she said. "He went off like a sky-rocket! One of the Dayton boys has gone after him; but he was running like all possessed when he went by their place, and we never shall see him again."

The boys asked for water, which she brought in a tin dipper, with a trembling hand. It was cold from the shoemaker's pump; and, having drunk, and thanked her, and condoled with the worthy couple for their loss, they resumed their tramp, without deeming it necessary to proclaim their own personal and peculiar interest in the many-times-sold dog.

Cliff laughed as they hurried along the village street.

"My ownership, that seemed so plain at the start," said he, "is getting to be like the road the traveler followed in the woods: first a wagon-track, then a cattle-path, then it dwindled to a squirrel-track and ran up a tree! Even if we catch the dog, I don't see what we are going to do with the claims of all these other people."

"We won't worry about that trouble till we get to it," Quint replied. "Dog or no dog, one owner or twenty, Algernon Knight Winslow is our game!"

XV

ADVENTURES BY THE WAY

HEY had not proceeded far beyond the village when they descried a youngster coming toward them, heated as if he had been running. He carried his hat in his hand, and at sight of Cliff and Quint grinned from ear to ear.

"That 's the Dayton boy; what 'll you bet?" said Cliff. And he called out, while the youngster was still some rods away, "Where 's the shoemaker's dog?"

"In Jericho, I guess!" laughed the youngster.

"Could n't you catch him?"

"Ketch him! Ye might as well try to ketch the shadder of a wild goose flyin' over a stump-lot!"

"You are my style of boy," said Quint, pleased with the youngster's wit. "Are all the village boys as bright as you are?"

"I don't know about *bright*," replied the youngster, "but I can run as fast as any of 'em, and I ain't goin' to run my legs off for anybody's dog."

"I would n't," said Quint. "Legs before dogs. Your

95

two are worth any four of the best dog in the world. We 've been traveling since morning," he added, hurrying on, while the youngster turned and stared after them; "and we have n't seen a dog that was worth chasing. We 'd like to!" he called back over his shoulder.

"See here," cried the youngster; "I 'll go a piece with you, if you 'll help me ketch him. Mrs. Ball said she 'd give half a dollar."

"That 's tempting," replied Cliff; "but we 've business of our own; can't attend to other people's."

And the Dayton youngster again turned toward the village.

The chase had become exciting, and our Biddicut boys gave little heed to the circumstance that it was taking them farther and farther from home.

"Winslow will be waiting somewhere for Sparkler to come up with him," Quint observed; "then he 'll be trying to sell him again; so we shall be gaining on him all the while."

Soon a team overtook them—a real "team" this time, consisting of a span of horses harnessed to an empty and clattering farm-wagon. The wayfarers turned up sweaty and appealing faces to the driver, and, drawing rein, he invited them to "hop in."

They climbed the wheel, and he made room for them on his seat—a board laid across the top of the rude wagon-box. It was a welcome change to the boys, enabling them not only to rest their limbs, but also to get over the road faster than they could have done on foot.

Their story amused the driver, who knew the last purchaser of the dog, the worthy shoemaker Ball. He carried them a mile or more, and would gladly have taken them farther; but, coming to a cross-road, they were afraid to go on without first assuring themselves as to the way the fugitives had taken.

They looked for dog-tracks on the crossings, and found several; but these seemed to indicate that the dog himself had hesitated there, and taken a turn or two before proceeding. Cliff was on fire with impatience.

"Is n't it too bad to lose time this way, when every minute is worth so much to us!" he exclaimed, almost inclined to blame Quint's too careful deliberation.

"No use fretting," said Quint, stooping over the faint footprints. "It may save time in the end to lose a little here. 'Be sure you 're right, then go ahead,' is a good motto; though most people prefer 'Go ahead, and guess at it.'"

"That 's more my way," Cliff acknowledged. "But think how far from Biddicut we are already, and really no nearer that dog than when we started! Hello!" he exclaimed, at sight of a yoke of oxen approaching on one of the cross-roads.

Beside the oxen walked a driver, his whip on his shoulder, and the short lash dangling over the near ox's horns.

"I 've just been to return a borrowed hay-cart," he explained, in answer to Cliff's interrogatories. "I must have been near an hour going and coming and talking, and I have n't seen any such man or dog."

"That means that they have kept straight on," said Quint.

"Just the way the man was carrying us!" said Cliff; "and we 've lost our ride and our time!"

"Things will happen so once in a while," Quint replied philosophically.

Five minutes later they perceived a small boy coming down a long slope of the road before them.

"He wants something," Cliff said presently. "He 's beckoning to us."

"And yelling," said Quint.

As they hastened on, the boy stopped in the middle of the road and waited for them.

"What is it, bub?" cried Quint.

"Are you the fellows that are hunting for a dog?" the small boy piped in a very small voice.

"Yes; have you seen him?" Cliff asked, with breathless eagerness.

"The man with the bag stopped at our house for a glass of milk," said the boy. "Then after a while the dog came along. We should n't have noticed him, only he run into the yard and out again, and snuffed around, as if he was following the man."

"That 's great news!" Quint exclaimed. "What angel sent you to tell us?"

"No angel! 't was my father," said the boy. "He 's the man that gave you a ride. He told me to come and find you."

With great glee the boys followed the small messenger back the way he came.

"'T was a judgmatical idea of Winslow's, that glass of milk!" observed Quint. "I should n't object to sampling the pan myself. I tell you, Cliff, there are worse things, when you are hungry and thirsty and in a hurry, than a glass of milk poured into a certain aperture I could mention!"

At the farm-house they met the man who had given them the ride, crossing his front yard to speak to them.

"I thought you ought to know," he said, as they thanked him for sending them the message. "By the way, would n't *you* like a glass of milk, or a bowl of milk, or a bowl of bread and milk?"

"That 's a remarkable coincidence!" said Quint. "I was just mentioning milk! Milk and I are very good friends."

"I 'm just sitting down to my dinner," said the farmer, "and I 'd like to have you join me. I guess we can give you a plate of b'iled victuals, if you have time to eat it."

"We should n't have time for that," Quint replied. "But bread and milk! What do you say, Cliff?"

"We are in an awful hurry," said Cliff; "but—such an offer as that!"

They did, however, take time to give their hands and faces a much-needed washing, and to brush their dusty clothes on the back porch. Meanwhile the farmer's daughters—two merry young girls, whose bright eyes made our Biddicut boys blush and feel awkward—placed brend and milk on the table opposite the single plate set for their father's late dinner, his family having dined in his absence.

"Do you think he'll feel hurt if I offer to pay him?" Cliff whispered to Quint, as they took their seats.

"He might; 't was an invitation. Better give the boy something for bringing us word," Quint suggested.

They were profuse in their thanks at parting; but the farmer said:

"You are quite welcome. If you come back this way, stop in. My name is Mills. You may want another bite by that time, and I shall want to hear how you make out dog-hunting."

"Was n't that bread and milk a godsend!" said Cliff, when they were once more on the road. "It may have to last till we get home to supper."

"Home to supper!" Quint replied, with a laugh. "I gave that up hours ago. We shall be lucky if our folks see us at breakfast-time to-morrow—or dinner! We're in for it, Cliff! Did you know it?"

"The worst of it is," said Cliff, "we're beginning to look like a couple of tramps; anyhow, that's the way I feel."

"Was it the pretty girls back there that made you feel so?" Quint queried.

"I could n't help looking at myself with their eyes, and wishing I had better clothes on," Cliff blushingly acknowledged.

"You 'll find your clothes are good enough for this job, before we get through with it," said Quint. "How much did you give the boy? I saw you slip something into his fist."

"Only a ten-cent piece," said Cliff. "I wanted to make it a quarter, but I 'm afraid we sha'n't have money enough to get home with."

"Winslow is our bank," replied Quint. "The farther we go, the more need there is of our catching him. We can't turn back!"

XVI

AN UNPLEASANT SURPRISE

HEY walked fast again, being sure of their trail, and soon got news of Winslow and the dog traveling together, but still a long distance ahead. They passed through another small village where he had offered Sparkler for sale, but without finding a purchaser.

After that it was easy to trace him; for as he went on through the well-settled but open country, he offered the dog to almost everybody he met, stopping to talk often; so that our Biddicut boys felt, at length, that they had him almost within view.

They were unaccustomed to such journeys. Their legs were beginning to ache; Cliff suffered from a pain in his side; Quint was unpleasantly reminded that he had a corn; and both discovered that bread and milk, and the few berries they picked by the wayside, were deficient in staying qualities as a diet. But now, inspired by the certain nearness of their game, they forgot soreness and fatigue; and Quint, whose breath held out better than Cliff's, proposed that they should try a trot.

"A *dog*-trot," he said, with a laugh. "Think you can stand it?"

"Yes, if my confounded side-ache does n't take me again," replied Cliff.

They set their hands to their hips, each with his coat hooked on one arm, and jogged on in silence, Quint always a pace or two ahead.

"I 'm getting my second wind," he said presently. "I feel more like running than I did two or three hours ago. Don't you?"

"Y-e-s!" said Cliff, admiring his companion's easy and steady lope. "We ought to get sight of 'em—from the top—of that knoll!"—speaking with difficulty.

"Hello!" said Quint, "there 's a crossing that 's going to bother us."

Crossings and forks were their chief source of delay and vexation, but for which they must have overtaken the fugitives long before. This one, however, hindered them hardly long enough to enable Cliff to recover breath. Fresh dog-tracks were discovered, and a little farther on they saw a man mowing briers by the roadside fence.

Yes; he had seen a man and a dog pass, ten or fifteen minutes before.

"Did he have a linen bag?"

"He had something; I did n't notice particular."

"Did he want to sell his dog?"

"No; he just asked how far it was to the Snelling farm.

That 's a great stock-farm, where they have all sorts of
live critters.　You can see it from the top of the hill
above here—a spread of buildings, with a tall windmill
and a red-painted water-tank."

Wild roses in bloom, and raspberry-bushes in full
bearing, were the briers the man was cutting.　The boys
hurriedly picked and ate berries while they talked.

"It seems too bad to cut those!" said Quint.

"They spread into the fields," replied the man.　"Wild
roses don't do no good, and I never git none of the berries."

He slashed away at the briers, while the boys hastened
on.

"'Wild roses don't do no good'!" Quint repeated dis-
dainfully; "and he cuts the raspberries because he 'never
gits none'!　A good man enough, I guess, but not exactly
my style."

He had cut off a spray of the wild roses, which he stuck
in his hat-band.　Cliff carried a raspberry branch, pluck-
ing and eating the berries as they pushed on.

They were soon at the summit of the hill, gazing down
upon a long stretch of open road, and near by, on the
left, the orchards and buildings and tall windmill of the
great Snelling farm.

"No such need of hurrying now," said Quint, wiping
his forehead.　"We must save our wind for emergencies.
If he 's there, he 'll stay till we come.　Then there 's no
knowing what will happen!"　He laughed grimly.

They put on their coats, and talked in low tones as they

walked, still at a brisk pace, under the shelter of some orchard-trees growing near the street.

"You look out for the dog; get hold of him the first thing, and leave me to deal with Winslow," said Quint. "Keep cool!"—for he saw that Cliff was excited.

They came in sight of the great granite posts of the Snelling gateway, before entering which they stopped to wait for a carriage coming toward them along the road beyond. The driver answered their concise inquiries without drawing rein. He had met no man and dog.

"Then he's here!" Quint said to his companion, as, with all their senses alert, they turned in at the open gate.

One branch of a broad driveway curved in toward the front of the house; the other led to the rear, and to the farm-buildings beyond. This the boys followed, keeping close to a thick border of Norway spruces, that thrust out heavy boughs above their heads. So they came to an open coach-house, in the doorway of which an old coachman in overalls was polishing the brass mountings of a handsome harness.

"Have you seen a man and a dog come into the place lately?" Cliff asked in a low voice, which he could n't keep from trembling.

"I have—not many minutes ago," replied the old coachman. "He inquired for Mr. Snelling, and they have just gone into the yards together."

"The yards? Where are they?"

"Right ahead; go through that gate." The old coachman stood at the door and pointed.

7

"Can't you go and show us?" said Quint, who felt that
the occasion had come for which they would have need of
all their wits and a course clear of uncertainties.

The old coachman dropped his polishing-brush on a
chair, dusted his fingers on his overalls, and said, "Come
along." The boys were careful to keep a little behind him
and partially concealed by his broad shoulders, as he
passed the gate and crossed a corner of the yard toward
an open shed between two barns. There was a sound of
voices in that direction, and presently the old man said:

"There's Mr. Snelling, patting the cow's neck; and
there's your man, with his dog."

The little group was in an angle of the shed, not twenty
yards away. The boys peered over the shoulders of their
guide, eager to command the situation, yet cautious of
exposing themselves to view. He had stopped; they
stopped too, in sudden amazement.

The man in the shed with Mr. Snelling was putting a
rope on the cow's horns. He was an Irish laborer, and
his dog was an ugly bull-terrier.

"Was n't there another man?" Cliff gasped out.

The old coachman had seen no other, and no other dog.
Quint felt himself dissolving in a clammy sweat; but he
soon recovered his equanimity, and questioned the Irish
laborer.

The man had been sent for the cow from a farm about
two miles away, and it appeared that he had come by the
cross-road at the corners of which the boys had last
stopped to look for tracks, and found them, although

"'THERE'S YOUR MAN, WITH HIS DOG.'"

they were probably those of the wrong dog. He had seen no such man and dog as Quint described.

"Well, Quint, what now?" said Cliff, with a sorry smile, almost ready to cry with disappointment and vexation.

"What time is it?" Quint asked, turning to the coachman, who pulled out a big silver watch and obligingly turned the full moon of its rimmed face toward the boys. "Thank you," said Quint. "Only half-past two. Earlier than I thought."

"We might get home to-night, if we start now," said Cliff. "We 've lost the trail."

"But we may pick it up again," replied Quint. "If you are tuckered out and discouraged, you can rest here, while I start out alone to make discoveries."

"If *you* keep on, *I* shall," said Cliff. "It was partly on your account I felt we ought to take the shortest cut home."

Quint answered, with one of his drollest smiles:

"As for me, I 'm just finding out what my gambrel-roof nose is for; it 's to follow through thick and thin the man who named it. Come on!"

XVII

AT THE STAR GROVE HOTEL

HE cook of the Star Grove Hotel was old and lame and cross, and she was put into a specially ill humor that afternoon by being called upon to broil a beefsteak for a late-arriving traveler.

"I 'll choose the toughest piece in the ice-chest," she declared, "and I 'll take care to spoil it over a poor fire." Then she proceeded to blow up her coals, select a juicy bit of sirloin, and prepare one of those delectable steaks for which she and the house were celebrated. With as many faults as a hedgehog has quills, she atoned for them all by her professional pride and skill.

"He 's just as pleasant as he can be," said light-footed Jenny Ray (a college girl turned waitress for the summer), coming from the dining-room after serving the traveler. "He told me to give this to the only cook he has struck since he has been in the States who knows how to broil a beefsteak."

110

The old woman had seated herself in the broad-roofed, open passage connecting the dining-room and the summer kitchen, and was cooling her flushed face and heated temper in the breeze that blew freshly through.

"Huh!" she ejaculated, scrutinizing the coin Jenny dropped into her hand. "'Since he has been in the States'? He's English, I'll be bound. The English are the only people in the world who know a good beefsteak. Yankees never think of feeing the cook, neither. What did he give *you*, Jenny?"

"The same," said the smiling waitress.

"He's an English gentleman!" the old woman declared. "Is there anything else he would like? There's a little of that sherbet left in the freezer. I thought I might need it myself by 'n' by, to cool my blood. But you can offer it to him."

The "English gentleman" *would* like the sherbet, and it was served accordingly.

"I hope he has come for the rest of the season," the old cook muttered to herself. "A gent that has money, and ain't afraid of parting with it, is the kind we'd like to see more samples of in a house like this. Well, what do *you* want?"

Two tired, dusty, forlorn-looking boys, whose appearance tallied ill with the description of guests she was wishing to see more of, came around a corner of the hotel, and stood waiting to have a word with her.

"We don't find anybody in the office," said the younger of the two.

"The office generally runs itself from now till the five-o'clock coach arrives," she replied. "What might you be wanting in the office?"

"We are looking for an acquaintance," said the older boy, who was also taller, and had a remarkably well-developed nose on a strong, honest face. "We thought he might have come to this hotel."

"He had on a loose-fitting brown coat, a little fuzz on his upper lip, and he had a dog with him, the last we heard," said the younger boy—Cliff Chantry, in short.

"There's been no such person here, with or without a dog," said the old .woman, sternly. "There's been no arrival this afternoon but an English gentleman, about an hour ago."

Cliff's face wore a hopeless expression; it seemed to him useless to pursue the inquiry. But Quint queried:

"An English gentleman?"

"An English gentleman!" she repeated haughtily. "He ain't the first one that's honored this house, and I hope he won't be the last. We had an English lord here once, and I'm thinking this is another."

Having said this, she gazed far away over the boys' heads at a landscape of green slopes and wooded hills, in the blue distance, appearing to have no interest in any nearer object within her range of vision.

That she was not to prove a fountain of obliging information was evident enough; but Quint said:

"Did he—your English lord—come afoot, and carry a linen gripsack, his shirt-collar just the least mite yellow about the edges?"

That brought her absent gaze back to the two figures in the foreground of her landscape. With her other excellent qualities, she possessed a bold imagination, to which she now gave free rein.

"He came in a carriage from the station, as the hotel coach did n't connect with that train. How many hand-bags or valises came with him, I don't know; but he has six trunks coming this evening. He engaged the two best rooms in the house by letter, and ordered a beefsteak by telegraph; he has just eaten it, and is finishing his sherbet. Not at all the sort of gentleman you claim as an acquaintance—yaller shirt-collar, indeed!"

The glowering look with which she said this discouraged further questions. The boys stepped aside for a brief consultation.

It was now two hours since they had lost Winslow's trail, and they had worn out their strength and patience in the vain endeavor to pick it up again. Even Quint was beginning to feel that it might have been better to accept Cliff's suggestion, abandon the quest, and start for home by the shortest cut from the Snelling farm. Since the bread and milk they had had at the Mills farm-house, they had tasted nothing but cold water and wayside berries, and they were faint with hunger.

At the close of their whispered consultation, Cliff said:

"You ask her. I can't; she's so thundering cross!"

"All right!" Quint replied. "She can't do more than bite my head off, and I'm beginning to think that is n't worth much."

He turned to the old woman.

"Beefsteaks and sherbet are not exactly in our line; but if you can give us a couple of sandwiches, we'll be glad to pay you for your trouble."

The old cook answered tartly:

"The Star Grove Hotel ain't a sandwich-shop, I'd have you know. There's a grocery in the village."

"How far away?" Quint inquired.

"Between here and the railroad deepo—about half a mile."

They took off their hats, thanking her with a politeness which was perhaps a trifle ironic, and Quint said to Cliff as they went away:

"Shall we go to the cracker-and-cheese shop she mentions, or what's your notion?"

"That girl looked as if she would have given us something, if it had n't been for the old one," said Cliff, regretfully. Jenny had come out in time to hear their parting words with the cook, regarding them with bright, sympathetic eyes. "But it's no use! We'll buy out the grocery, then find the soft side of a rock to sit on, and talk this thing over while we nibble."

"I gave them a string of yarns as long as a kite-tail!" the old woman chuckled, with malicious glee, as they disappeared around the corner of the hotel.

"Why did you?" said Jenny. "They seemed to be honest boys."

"Claiming any guest of this house as a friend of theirs, and asking for sandwiches!" scoffed the cook. "Of course they never expected to pay for 'em. An English lord!—he! he!—and six trunks!"

XVIII

"AN ENGLISH LORD WITH SIX TRUNKS"

EANWHILE the possible British nobleman strolled into the reading-room, where he picked his teeth and glanced at the newspapers for a few minutes; then he took a turn or two on the long hotel piazza, and finally came around to the roofed passage where the cook sat cooling her rotund visage in the breeze.

She was rather unpleasantly reminded of the two boys' description of their "friend," noticing the singular coincidence that this foreign tourist also had on a loosely fitting brown coat, and a shirt-collar yellowed about the edges.

In suavity of manner, however, he was all that Jenny's words and her own fancy had painted him. With an ingratiating smile, he inquired:

"Have you, madam, seen a stray dog about here while I have been in the dining-room?"

This was another remarkable coincidence. Without waiting for a reply, he proceeded glibly:

116

" Mine chased a squirrel into some woods back here, and I left him barking up a tree. He 'll turn up before long, —he generally does,—and he may want a piece of meat. Will you oblige me by having something ready for him when he puts in an appearance ? "

Nothing in his demeanor impelled her to address him as she would have been prepared to address a British nobleman ; but she remembered his generous fees, and answered promptly :

" All right, sir ! I 'll look out for him."

"Thanks ever so much !" he replied. " If he does n't find me the first thing, he 'll make for the kitchen door. That 's a rule of his—a moral principle." He laughed, and looked about him. " Your hotel is delightfully situated. That shady retreat is very inviting."

He walked back into the hotel, and presently reappearing with a light duster on, strolled off into the grove.

The old cook watched him with a curiously puzzled expression.

" An English lord with six trunks !" she repeated to herself, with a derisive titter. "I suppose I ought to have told him his friends are looking for him ; but that 's none of my business. See the cheek of him, now !" she suddenly exclaimed,—"stretching himself in Mrs. Mayhew's hammock, that she 's so awful particular about ! But that 's not my affair, either. I 've something else to think of, from now till supper-time."

And she waddled into the kitchen.

On their way to the grocery the boys noticed three or

four wagons halted on a side-street, and a group of men
and boys standing near one of them.

Although sick of the sound of their own voices putting
over and over again the same monotonous questions regarding a man and a dog, they still continued their inquiries at every opportunity; and Quint now observed:

"There's another good chance to make ourselves ridiculous; those teamsters may tell us something."

"The teamsters can wait; my appetite won't," replied
Cliff. "I'm going on a voyage of discovery to those
cracker-barrels!"

"There's a judgmatical streak somewhere in your
make-up," Quint said approvingly. "I'll enlist for that
voyage."

At the grocery Cliff called for ten cents' worth of plain
crackers, and was surprised to find how many so small an
outlay would procure. He then asked for three cents'
worth of cheese, and was a little ashamed of his stingi-
ness when he saw how small a lump the grocer wrapped
in brown paper and passed to him over the counter.

"Another three cents' worth!" he ordered munificently,
handing the first package to Quint, and receiving the
second for himself.

He also threw in his man-and-dog question, in a casual
sort of way, and not expecting to make anything by it, he
was n't disappointed.

They stuffed their pockets with the crackers, each re-
serving one for his hand; each had also his wedge of
cheese, bared of its brown-paper wrapper at the thin end,

convenient for being fed into the small mill of white teeth
alternately with bites of cracker.

"That was good advice the old woman gave us," said
Quint, "if only she had n't pitched it at us in that dis-
agreeable fashion! A good deal depends on the way a
thing is given—us Tim Oakes said when his sister flung
the squash-pie in his face. He had been teasing for
squash-pie, but!"—Quint stopped his own mouth with
his ration.

"This is better than a stone wall for a little rest," said
Cliff, seating himself on the grocery steps. "Here,
Quint!"

"I 'll let you do my share of the sitting," Quint replied.
"I 'm going to pump those teamsters. If I don't hear
anything encouraging, then I shall conclude Winslow has
struck the railroad and left this part of the country."

"I shall feel mean, sitting here while you go about my
business," said Cliff; "but I don't feel as if—I—could—
stir!"

Quint crammed into his mouth the last fragment of
cracker he was engaged upon, as he turned down the side
street and approached the blockade of wagons. For a
blockade it was, by this time. He thought he had n't
seen so many vehicles in all the afternoon, and he wondered where they had come from. Still another was just
arriving.

XIX

THE HOT BOX

"ELLO!" cried the driver, "what's the joke?"

"Hot box," came the reply from the group of bystanders. And he, too, jumped down from his wagon, a light carryall, and joined them.

Quint followed, and saw with his own eyes what the trouble was. An axle-box of a heavy draft-wagon loaded with wood had become heated by friction, and the wheel had ceased to revolve. It would be some time before the metal would cool and shrink sufficiently to relieve the hub; even then, without oil, it would heat again before the wagon could go far. In these circumstances it was interesting to observe the brotherly cheerfulness with which the other teamsters came to the assistance of the one in difficulty.

It was a rear wheel, and three men were lifting that corner of the load by means of a plank used as a lever. Two others were swinging upon the wheel thus raised a few inches from the ground, while the one they were aiding gripped the spokes opposite the hub. One of the bystanders was holding a stick and a pot of grease, ready to give the axle the necessary oiling as soon as it should be exposed.

Seeing the wheel loosening a little, Quint also laid hold of the spokes, and, forgetting how weary he was from his all-day tramp, helped pull it off.

"You 've got a pretty good grip in them hands!" the teamster said to him. "I 'm much obliged to everybody."

Then, while the oil was being applied, Quint introduced his own business to a remarkably well-disposed audience. The driver of the light carryall, who was returning to his vehicle, stopped to listen, and remarked:

"Your man was a slim-waisted party, not above three or four and twenty, narrow in the lower part of his mug —a sort of pinched look right here?"—with thumb and fingers pressing the sides of his own chin.

"That 's the chap!" Quint exclaimed.

"And the dog—he had short brown curly hair—looked like some kind of a spaniel? had on a collar with nickel-headed brads in it?"

"The very dog!" cried Quint.

"That party," said the driver of the light carryall, "begged a ride of me this afternoon, and took his dog with him into the wagon."

From the information he proceeded to give, Quint concluded that Winslow and Sparkler had been taken up not far from the crossing where he and Cliff lost track of them

and got upon the trail by which they had been so woe-
fully misled. The driver of the light carryall had come
from that direction, and was now on his way back.

"How far did you carry them?" Quint inquired.

"Maybe a couple of miles in this direction, and then
half a mile off on the Fulton road, where I had business
with a man by the name of Ames. I left your chap there
trying to sell his dog. I am driving right back in that
direction. I can take you along and show you the house."

"I jump at that!" Quint exclaimed. "Only wait till I
can speak to my chum!"

Cliff, as he confessed afterward, was feeling that he
could never get up from those grocery steps, when Quint
came hurrying toward him with the exciting news. He
was off the steps in an instant, quite forgetting that he had
ever known fatigue, and in three minutes they were rid-
ing away with their new friend.

He was sociable, and had a good deal to say about
Winslow, among other things this:

"Before he got into my wagon, he took a long, glossy
brown duster out of his bag, whipped the dust from his
shoulders with it, and then put it on over his coat. There
did n't seem to be much left in his bag, so he just made a
roll of it, which he held in his lap or under his arm. His
dog lay in the wagon-bottom, where he would n't be much
noticed."

"That accounts for our losing trace of them so suddenly," said Cliff; "for we made inquiries all along that
road."

They related their adventures, and Quint asked the driver if he knew the Mills farm-house, where they were treated to bread and milk, and got laughed at by two pretty girls.

"I rather think I do!" the man replied, with a broadening smile. "My name is Putney. If you had mentioned it, those girls might have told you I courted my wife in that house. She is their eldest sister."

The boys were delighted to hear this, and went on praising the hospitality of the Mills household in a way that caused their new friend to warm to them more and more.

"It is n't over three quarters of a mile from my house to theirs, across country," he said. "Now, I 'll tell you what I 'll do. I 'll drive you to Ames's. Then, if you find you 've missed your man again, and don't see much chance of catching him or the dog, I 'll put you on the way to my father-in-law's, where I advise you to pass the night; or I 'll keep you over myself. Then you can start out fresh in the morning."

The boys were touched by the kindness of this proposal, and impressed by the wisdom of the advice. To Cliff particularly it seemed as if it would be the most blissful thing imaginable to settle down in some quiet farm-house for the night, talk over their adventures after a good supper, and then go to bed; he felt, as he told Quint afterward, as if he would like to sleep about forty hours out of the next twenty-four. He almost hoped that, if they did n't come upon Winslow or Sparkler, they might

8

not get any encouraging news of them, so that they
would n't feel obliged to bestir themselves further in that
thankless business.

The road was smooth, the country pleasant, the sun
low, and the air cool, and the boys were enjoying greatly
their restful mode of travel, when Quint suddenly threw
up his hands and uttered a startling cry :

"There ! Look ! Hold on ! "—at the same time making
an instinctive clutch at the reins.

Cliff looked, and saw before them, coming on the roadside, running fast, a dog—the dog they sought,—there
could be no doubt of it,—Sparkler !

XX

A MEETING AND A PARTING

"OH, by Jehu!" Cliff exclaimed. "Stop
him! stop him!"

Whether he meant "stop the horse"
or "stop the dog," he himself could n't
have told. He probably meant both.
Before the wagon came to a halt, the
boys tumbled themselves down over wheel and foot-board,
and rushed, with outstretched hands, to head off the fugitive. Sparkler was running directly toward them; and
Cliff almost hoped for a moment that his pet was hasten-
ing to meet him, as eager for a reunion as he was!

But the dog's conduct quickly dispelled that fond fancy.
There dangled from his collar just such a piece of cord as
he started with in the morning, as if he had been running
with it all day. He passed so near that Cliff actually
reached down to clutch it, at the same time calling and
coaxing, "Sparkler! Come, Sparkler!" when the animal
turned suddenly aside, darted by the horse's legs, escaped
under the wagon, and was rods away before the boys were
fully aware what had happened.

"That's the dog!" said Mr. Putney.

"Of course it is!" cried Cliff, wildly excited.   "He has been sold again!"

"And has gnawed his rope," said Quint.

"What will you do?" their new friend asked.   "Follow him, or drive on with me and see if you can find his master?"

"His master has gone in the direction the dog has," said Quint.   "Following one, we follow both."

"We can trace the dog easier now, as we did in the morning, with the flying piece of cord to attract attention," cried Cliff, once more full of the ardor of pursuit.

"Sorry to bid you and your carryall good-by, Mr. Putney," said Quint; "but you see how it is."

"I'd turn about and drive you a piece, if my horse had n't been so long on the road," Mr. Putney replied. "If you find it convenient to come to my house, or my father-in-law's,"—he raised his voice as they were hurrying away,—"you'll be welcome!"

They shouted back their thanks as they ran.

The tide of human life, which had been at its lowest ebb when the Biddicut boys first touched at the Star Grove Hotel, was by this time rising again in and about that favorite summer resort.

Old ladies, refreshed by their afternoon siestas, came from their rooms to the breezy piazzas, where they grouped themselves on benches and chairs, or took gentle exercise by walking to and fro beneath the broadly projecting roof; young ladies with parasols and books strolled

in from the woods and berry-fields; and a boisterous party
of excursionists returned, alighting with chatter and
laughter at the hotel steps. Then the five-o'clock coach
arrived, bringing passengers from the train. The clerk
was busy at the desk; the housekeeper was showing new
boarders their rooms; and the cook was storming in the
kitchen, to the terror of the young waitresses.

"Where's my maid?" cried a bustling and important
woman, sweeping along the piazza. "Where's Betsy?
Betsy!"—as the maid appeared, trundling a baby-carriage,—"who is that man lounging in my new hammock?
Why do you allow such a thing as that?"

"How could I help it, ma'am?" said Betsy. "I had
been getting the children washed, after their play in the
sand, and when I went out, there he was, asleep on the
cushions; and what could I do?"

"Go at once!" commanded the lady—"say you have
orders to take the hammock in, as its owner thinks it is
going to rain. Say it is Mrs. Mayhew's private property."

Betsy went reluctantly to obey the order, while her
mistress stayed with the baby-carriage.

"Dear me!" Mrs. Mayhew suddenly exclaimed, "what
dog is that? How strangely he acts! Don't dare to
touch him, Philip! He may be mad."

The dog, just arrived, had a short piece of cord attached to his collar, and he was acting strangely indeed.
There was n't the slightest danger of Philip Mayhew or
any other boy touching him, although two or three were
soon trying to lay hold of the cord.

He ran in at the door and out again, darted between two of his pursuers, who bumped heads as he slipped through their fingers, capered around the corner of the hotel toward the kitchen, occasionally dropping his nose to the ground, and finally ran into the grove, where he jumped joyously upon the trousers of the stranger, who, at Betsy's request, was just then rolling out of the hammock.

"That your dog, mister?" cried Philip.

"He is mine—he is everybody's; at least, everybody seems to think so. What were you boys chasing him for?" said the stranger.

"I thought he had got away from somebody; I saw the rope on his neck," replied Philip.

"That cord is very useful in the performance of one of his favorite tricks," said the owner, with a peculiar laugh, stooping, however, and quickly removing the cord from the dog's collar. "He can do things that will astonish you. If enough of the boarders were interested, I could show you—right here in the grove, or on the hotel piazza —what a wonderful dog he is."

"Show us his tricks! Oh, mister, show us some of his tricks!" clamored the boys.

"Get some men—some ladies—somebody that can appreciate the most intelligent canine creature in the world," said the owner, looking around on his not very satisfactory audience of nurses and children.

"We can appreciate him!" cried the boys. "One trick, mister!"

Just then the hotel gong sounded.

"There 's your supper," said the owner, with a shrug of the shoulders. "It 's no use now. Perhaps after supper—" He stooped again and caressed the dog. "Look alive, now ! "

The animal sat up immediately, raising his fore paws, to the delight of the boys and nurses.

"What do you want ?   Food ?"

The dog made no motion, but watched his master with bright, intelligent eyes.

"No; he has been fed, and so have I.   Walk ?—take a walk ?"   The dog dropped one of his lifted paws.   "That means yes; he would like to take a walk and see something of the beautiful country around here.   I approve of his judgment.   You see what sort of a prodigy he is, and you 'll know what to expect if I am back here in time to show you some of his tricks this evening."

So saying, he walked off through the grove, while the boys, who would have much preferred a performance by the dog to the old cook's most inviting supper, watched the two disappear, and returned reluctantly to the hotel.

About half an hour after this our two Biddicut boys came panting up the Star Grove driveway.   They had had more trouble than they anticipated in following Sparkler, having lost track of him in consequence of an unexpected turn he had made, and then learned, to their bewilderment, that such a dog had been seen going toward the very hotel they had so lately visited.

Eager to verify this report, they dashed up the piazza

steps, and met the office-clerk in the doorway. Yes, he said; a dog with a cord hanging from his collar had been dodging about there a little while ago, and he had last seen him running around the corner of the hotel, pursued by some boys.

Where were the boys? At supper. Which corner of the hotel? He told them, and a minute later Quint and Cliff were standing on the spot where they had interviewed the crusty-tempered old cook.

The cook was no longer there; but presently Jenny Ray appeared, bearing some dishes on a tray, between the dining-room and the kitchen. She recognized them, and smiled at their question.

"The dog was here only a little while ago," she informed them, "and I believe the man himself was in the dining-room at the very time you were inquiring for him."

"The English lord!" exclaimed Cliff.

Jenny laughed till she was near spilling the dishes off her tray.

"The cook told me how she fibbed to you," she replied. "It was too bad!" Yet she seemed to think it very funny.

"I'd like to fan her with her own gridiron!" said Quint. "What a chance she made us lose! Where is he now—the man?"

"I don't know; he was in the grove till his dog came and found him. But I must go now!" And Jenny disappeared in the kitchen.

The boys hastened to the grove, where they found a

"'THE DOG WAS HERE ONLY A LITTLE WHILE AGO.'"

nurse with two small children, and learned from her that
Winslow had gone off with his dog shortly after the sup-
per-gong sounded.

"Which way did he go?" Cliff asked excitedly.

She showed the way Winslow had taken through the
grove, and Cliff was for following immediately; but Quint
had a question to ask:

"How was the fellow dressed?"

"I did n't notice, except that he had on something like
a gauze waterproof."

"Did he carry a bag?"

"I did n't notice any. He spoke of coming back and
showing off the dog's tricks to the boarders this evening."

"He wore his duster," Quint said to Cliff. "I wish I
knew about his bag. Shall I run over and see if he has
left it at the hotel?"

"I don't think we ought to lose a minute!" Cliff declared. "She says he spoke of coming back; for that
reason I don't think he means to be seen here again. If
we start right off we may overtake him, or meet him if he
does come back."

"Start it is, then!" said Quint.

XXI

THE WAYSIDE SHED

 DRIVEWAY skirting the grove in the rear of the hotel led to an open road not far beyond. This the boys soon struck, and were fortunate in hearing of Winslow and the dog before much time was lost in looking for tracks.

They found themselves on a beautiful upland, with the grove on their left, a rolling farm region on the other side, and before them a pleasant road stretching away to the westward, across a cool valley, toward distant wooded hills. The sun was not yet set, but masses of black cloud with wondrously illumined edges, surging up in a wild sky, cast a strange gloom over all the landscape.

There was a lurid light in the boys' faces as they looked at each other without slackening their rapid pace.

"There's rain-water in that cloud," said Quint, "and thunder and lightning. I've felt a storm brewing all the afternoon."

"Do you believe it will come here?" Cliff asked.

"If it keeps on the way it is moving, we shall get it," Quint replied. "The lightning is having a circus!"—as the black face of the cloud crinkled with sudden flashes.

At no time during the day had they felt more certain hope of coming up with their game. If Winslow did not turn back on his course, or lose time by offering Sparkler for sale, and so allow them to gain upon him, he must soon, they reasoned, seek shelter from the coming storm; and they determined not to pass a wayside house without stopping to make inquiries.

These stops caused some delay; but they succeeded in keeping his trail, and came at length to a gloomy hollow, where there was a solitary farm-house a little back from the street, and an open wagon-shed on the roadside. A young man was crossing a barn-yard behind the shed, when they accosted him. Yes; he had seen just such a man as they described, with just such a dog, go by a little while before.

"Does n't the road fork right here?" Quint asked, pointing forward into the deepening gloom.

"Yes; the left-hand road goes over the hills; the lower one keeps the level country to Burbeck."

"Could you see which he took?"

"No; I did n't notice after he passed the gate." And, after answering some further questions, the man went on into the barn.

So it happened that when the boys reached the fork they were again puzzled, as they had been similarly, so many times, in the course of that dubious adventure.

Although it was not yet night, the shadow of the advancing storm was gathering so fast that they would hardly have been able to detect footprints, even if any had been impressed in the hard, gravelly road-bed.

"Well, what now, Quint?" said Cliff, his face showing pale and anxious in a gleam of lightning which just then lit up the landscape.

"I 'll go ahead on this left-hand road, which shows most travel," Quint replied, "while you wait here, or perhaps go as far as the first house on the other branch. Whether we find out anything or not, we 'll both come back here; and the one that comes first will wait for the other under that shed; that will be as good a shelter as any, when the storm breaks."

A feeling of dread came over Cliff at the thought of parting from his friend, even for a brief interval, at such a crisis. The increasing darkness, the dazzling lightning, the far-off, tumbling thunder, rolling ever nearer, and the utter loneliness of their strange surroundings, filled him with indefinable forebodings. His was a more imaginative nature than Quint's. The murmur of a little wayside brook warned him of fearful things impending; while Quint, in the most matter-of-fact manner, bent down to scoop up water in his palms, and quench his thirst with it, before starting on again.

But Cliff, too, was brave and resolute, and, without breathing a syllable of his shuddering apprehensions, he acceded to Quint's plan. So they separated at the fork, and hurried on their diverging ways, bushy and hilly

fields soon intervening to hide each from the other's
view.

Cliff had not gone far before he came to a farm-house,
where he was assured no such man as he inquired for had
been seen. A little farther on he met a wagon, the driver
of which pulled up his horse reluctantly, shook his head
sullenly, and, with an anxious look at the sky, whipped
on again.

Cliff did not stop long to consider what he should do.
A dazzling, zigzag rift, running across the blackness of
the heavens, followed by an appalling crash of thunder
and splashes of rain, put an end to all irresolution.

"By Jehu!" he exclaimed aloud, with thrills of fear
crawling all over him, "I am going back!"

He hoped to find Quint in the shed before him; but it
was empty. It was a most desolate place, but he was glad
to have a roof between him and the lightning-riven sky
and bursting thunder. He stood in the great opening,
and looked out, straining his eyes in the obscurity or
winking at the glare, and listening for footsteps, caring
little now for Winslow, but longing for Quint to come.
He seemed to think that, whatever happened, it would n't
be half so bad if his friend were present. Such comfort
is companionship in times of trouble!

The rain, after a few fitful dashes, held off unaccount-
ably; there was even a lifting of the gloom at one time,
showing that it was not yet night, as he had begun to
fear, and deluding him with the hope that the storm was
passing by.

He explored the shed. At one end was an old tip-cart, while nearer the center was a farm-wagon, run in diagonally, with the neap pushed into the vacant corner, over a manger at the rear. He discovered, to his satisfaction, that the manger contained a litter of straw.

"When Quint comes," he said, "we can camp down here, out of the rain. Not at all a bad place to pass a wet night! If only he would come!"

As the manger would be too narrow for them both, he gathered up the straw and made a bed of it on the ground against the end of the shed. Then again he stood in the opening, looking, listening, longing for his friend. Suddenly came the sound of heavy drops pattering on the roof and the ground without. A wind was rising, and the gusts blew whiffs of spray into his face, causing him to draw farther back beneath the roof.

"Wishing won't fetch him, and worrying won't do any good," he said; and yielding to a sense of overpowering weariness, he got down upon his bed of straw.

He remembered how often, under the attic roof at home, he had been lulled to rest by the mild music of the wind and rain. Something like the same influence stole over him now, and he thought what comfort it would be to cuddle down there with his friend, forget Winslow and Sparkler and all anxiety and care, and sink into blissful slumber!

But where, all the while, was Quint?

It was darker again, but still light enough for him to perceive anybody that might be passing on the road.

He still thought of Winslow, but his chief solicitude was to see the tall, lank form of his friend appear at the opening. Had some accident happened to him? What could keep him so long? It had not rained hard at first, but now the volleys came down with a rushing sound.

He tried to console himself with the reflection that Quint had sought shelter in some farm-house; but that would n't be like Quint. Then his mind reverted to their folks at home, his own mother talking of him at that very moment, and hearkening for his footsteps in the rain.

"I know she won't sleep a wink all night," he said to himself, remorsefully. "What a fool I have been, and what a scrape I have got Quint into! But it *would* have been a satisfaction to do what our dads did n't believe we could—catch Winslow or the dog—and I thought—"

All at once the tired boy stopped thinking altogether. A whole procession of dogs and Winslows might have passed; Quint's mysterious absence, his own pains and fatigues and disappointments, thunder and lightning and wind and rain—he was sweetly oblivious of all, fast asleep on his straw.

XXII

"WHAT DO YOU WANT OF ME?"

UINT proceeded some distance on his branch of the forked road, making fruitless inquiries at farm-houses, and meeting no travelers. All he expected to do was to determine whether Winslow had taken that route, and he was unwilling to turn back before satisfying himself on that point. At length he came to a cross-road presenting the usual difficulties, and he perceived the uselessness of keeping on.

"Cross-roads, I should say!" he muttered, as he stood and gazed off in the three directions, either one of which Winslow might have taken. "They make *me* cross enough. Well, that 's rather sharp!"

"That" was a frightful flash of lightning, with its quickly following peal—probably the same that decided Cliff to return to the shelter of the shed. Still Quint stood deliberating, holding out his hand to catch the raindrops.

It was a lonely situation, surrounded by barren and

"FACING EACH OTHER IN THAT TERRIBLE SOLITUDE."

bushy fields, except on one side, where a clump of dark woods straggled down to the very corner of the cross-roads. He stood among the scattered trees,—stunted oaks and hard pines,—and strained his every nerve to watch and listen.

He was on the point of turning reluctantly back when he heard quick footsteps, and presently perceived, a little way before him, the figure of a man walking fast in the middle of the road. Quint stepped out from the wayside to accost him.

"Good evening, stranger," he began, and stopped.

No need to put the inquiry that was on his lips. No need of the lightning-flash that just then flooded heaven and earth, and poured its white instantaneous glare on the two human figures facing each other in that terrible solitude.

Despite the long gray duster, or gauze waterproof, in which the form of the stranger was partly disguised, Quint had already, in the unillumined gloom, recognized the man he and Cliff had been all day pursuing.

The other was slower to identify his old acquaintance.

"Not quite so good an evening as it might be," he replied, without pausing in his hurried walk until Quint stepped immediately before him. Then came the flash, bringing out in startling distinctness the pale, earnest, prominent features of the boy who had waylaid him.

"Hello!" said the dog-seller, skipping aside with an exceedingly alert movement, very much as if he had been stopped by a highwayman. "What do you want of me?"

9

XXIII

QUINT CHOOSES HIS COMPANION

UINT also took a step, so that he still confronted him.

"You know pretty well what I want! I see you remember me!"

"Remember you!" cried Winslow, with a light laugh. "Brutus—or Cassius?—which is it? Brutus, I believe. Well, Marcus Brutus, what can I do for you? This is really like meeting an old friend!"

"Glad you think so," said Quint, in a low voice, and with a countenance that showed portentously stern and determined.

He had many times rehearsed to himself what he would do and say upon the chance of falling in with Winslow, but the present occasion was so different from any he had foreseen that he hardly knew how he alone was to deal with him.

But his wits did not desert him. Cliff was too far away to be called to his assistance; he must, then, try to take Winslow to Cliff.

"If you don't object," he said, "I 'll walk along with you."

"All right!" said Winslow. "But you seemed to be going in the opposite direction."

"You were going in that direction, too, a short time ago," said Quint, falling in by his side.

"I was out for a little walk," said Winslow; "now I am going back."

"Just my case," said Quint. "I was out for a walk, and now I am going back."

"And I 've got to hurry, for I don't care to get wet," said Winslow, quickening his step.

"Just my case every time," said Quint, keeping at his side. "I don't fancy a wetting."

"I shall be drenched before I get back to the Star Grove Hotel, if I don't run for it!" And Winslow broke into a light trot.

"That 's a nice house—worth running for," observed Quint, always within easy clutching distance of the dog-seller's right arm. And he calculated, with secret glee, that their present rate of speed would in five minutes bring them to the shed where Cliff would soon be, if he was n't there already.

It seemed as if Winslow must have read his mind; he was certainly suspicious of Quint's too evident willingness to accompany him in that direction. All at once he stopped.

"It is too far," he said. "It will pour before I can get half-way there. I am going back to a house I passed just before I saw you."

"There's a house only a little farther on," replied Quint; "and just beyond the forks of the road is a shed we can wait under till the shower is over."

Winslow turned and faced him with a sarcastic grin.

"The shed would n't be big enough for us both. I am going back."

"I 'm afraid it will be lonesome there without you; guess I 'll go back too"; and, turning as Winslow turned, Quint still kept close by his side.

"Now, look here, young man," cried Winslow; "this is a great country—big as all outdoors! It almost seems as if there was room in it for me and you and your gambrel-roof nose without crowding!"

"My nose and I will try not to crowd you," Quint answered. "But the fact is, poor company is better than none on such a night as this."

"My amiable friend," cried Winslow, his tones growing hard and sharp and menacing, "does n't it appeal to your common sense that a person has a right to choose his own company in this land of the free and home of the brave?"

"That 's just what I think," said Quint, "and I choose yours."

For a moment Winslow made no response, as he walked fast back toward the crossing, Quint's elbow constantly close to his own.

Quint would have yelled for Cliff, but he was n't sure Cliff was within hearing, and he hoped Winslow would yet conclude to return to the Star Grove Hotel. Upon one thing the boy from Biddicut was fully determined—

to stick to him until, with or without Cliff's assistance, he had got back Cliff's money. The dog was not with his master, but Quint cared little now for that often-sold animal.

Their hurried footsteps were the only sounds on that lonely road; but now and then the thunder tumbled down the cloudy crags of heaven, and the leaping lightning severed the gloom of the storm and night. On reaching the wooded corner, Winslow turned sharply on his unwelcome companion.

"I'm inclined to the opinion," he said, "that it's about time for you and me to come to some sort of an understanding."

"This seems to be a good place for it," Quint replied, sternly regarding him. "We need n't be afraid of an interruption."

"Then have the kindness to inform me just why you dog my footsteps in this way," said Winslow, threateningly.

"Because I can't *dog* them in any other," Quint replied. "I'm not a Sparkler."

"I see the point," remarked Winslow. "State your case, and we'll settle it on the spot—if not in one way, then in another. A very good spot, as you say!"

"You know the case perfectly well," said Quint, without heeding the threat. "You go about the country selling that dog. You have sold him once too often. That's my case, Mr. Algernon Knight Winslow!"

"I never sold him to you," Winslow retorted, insolent and defiant. "You are not Cassius."

"Cassius and I are solid in this business," said Quint.

"Well, name your terms!"

"The terms you proposed yourself, and put your name to; nothing more nor less. You 've given me and my friend a deal of trouble. You have got back your dog; now we want our money."

"How much?" Winslow asked, as coolly as if he had been prepared to hand out millions.

All the while the rain was slowly pattering, and the lightning was winking at them, as they confronted each other on the edge of the lonely woods.

For a moment Quint had hopes of bringing the dog-seller to an easy settlement.

"You remember the agreement. We gave you ten dollars. I want twenty." And he held out his hand.

"Was that the bargain? Show me the paper you say I signed. Business is business," said Winslow.

"Come with me," Quint replied, "and I 'll show you the paper in the presence of witnesses."

"Bring on your witnesses; I 'll wait here," said Winslow, stepping under the trees on the dreary roadside, and placing his back against one of the largest trunks.

XXIV

A DESPERATE ENCOUNTER

UINT also stepped aside under the trees, and stood facing him.

The dark woodland beyond looked impenetrably dense until lighted up by a vivid flash that showed each silent trunk distinct in its space, and quiet saplings ranged on each side of a broken and ruined wayside wall. The utter solitude, the surrounding desolation, the fitful gleams and peals, the on-coming night and storm, might well have tried the nerves of one older and more experienced than Quint; but no one could have been more determined.

"I can wait here as long as you can," he said; coolly adding, "I don't think there 's going to be much of a shower."

"Suppose we have a little frank talk," said Winslow. "We may as well take it easy; here 's a seat."

He moved to a fallen tree-trunk and sat down upon it. Quint guessed there was room for two, and sat down beside him.

"How long have you been following me?" The dog-seller's tone was quite friendly now.

"All day," Quint replied. "We've been only an hour or two behind you."

"Who is *we*?" queried Winslow.

"You may as well know; the fellow you sold the dog to—Cassius, as you call him. He is with me."

"I don't see him."

"No; he took another road, so as to head you off. He and I have been on the war-path ever since the dog got away this morning."

"Seems to me you are giving yourselves a deal of trouble for a small matter," Winslow remarked sarcastically.

"It's no small matter to us, let me tell you!" Quint replied. "Ten dollars is a big sum to a poor country boy. It's more than my chum had saved up in all his life; that's why he borrowed of me. Now, we are bound to have it back, with something for our trouble."

"You are a precious pair of country bumpkins!" laughed Winslow. "But I rather like your pluck. Come, now; be reasonable. What will you settle for?"

"Twenty dollars," Quint responded in his most direct and quiet tone of voice.

"That's absurd! I have n't got so much money as that."

"You've got more than that, Mr. Winslow. Before you sold that dog to us, you sold him to Mr. Miller, in the town of Wormwood. To-day you sold him first to an

old shoemaker, then again to somebody else, just before
you went to the Star Grove Hotel; and you 've sold him
again this evening."

"You 've kept the run of it pretty well; allow me to
compliment you!" jeered Winslow.

"How many more times you have sold him," Quint
went on, "you know better than I do. You certainly
have money; and the best thing in the world for you,
Mr. Winslow, is to fork out mine."

"What! you, an honest Biddicut boy, will receive
money got by fraud, as you claim?"

"I will," replied Quint, "even if I have to return a
part of it to those I know you have swindled. I have no
scruples at all about taking our share." And he looked
squarely at the dog-seller over the four feet of pine log
intervening between them.

"And what if I decline to give up to you my hard-
earned profits?" sneered Winslow.

"Then I 'll see that you don't earn any more in that
way; I 'll see that you are put where even your dog can't
find you! That 's the size of it, Mr. Winslow."

The dog-seller laughed derisively.

"You imagine you can make people believe your absurd
story? I deny every word of it. I never sold you and
Cassius a dog. I never sold anybody a dog. My dog is
not for sale; he is with my mother in Michigan. Besides,
I never had a dog. If you have a paper signed by my
name, it 's a forgery. I don't sign my name to papers.
More than all that, my name is n't Winslow."

He rattled this off with bewildering volubility, and taking a knife from his pocket, opened it with a peculiar motion, and began to stick the blade into the log they sat on—merely to display his weapon, Quint thought. It was not so dark but that he could see that the blade was long and bright. He also took out his knife and began to stab the log.

"It's funny, then," he said, "what we have hunted you all day for!"

"I know what for!" cried Winslow. "For blackmail. You have trumped up false charges against me, and think you'll force me to buy you off. That's what I say, and what I'll maintain."

"And the other people you've swindled,—I know just where to find some of them,—how will it be when they come to tell their story?" Quint demanded.

"Brutus," said the dog-seller, snapping his knife and putting it into his pocket, "I'll give you five dollars, and you shall go your way, and I'll go mine."

Quint quietly closed and pocketed his own knife, and answered dryly:

"You submit to 'blackmail'?"

"I'll submit to anything for a dry skin." The rain had held off, but it was beginning to patter again. "We're a couple of fools to sit here and palaver, when our little affair can be compromised so easily."

"So I think; but five dollars won't compromise it," said Quint.

"Very well, then!" exclaimed Winslow, a blaze of

lightning showing a sinister resolution in his keen face;
"we 'll sit it out. I 've got on a waterproof; I can stand
it, if you can."

"I 've got a better waterproof than that," said Quint,
with ominously set lips. "I 'm going to get mad by and
by; that will keep me from caring for the weather.
You 'd better not put off settling too long."

The rain came down in big drops. The thunder was
terrific. Then, between the peals, a rushing and roaring
sound could be heard, distant and faint at first, then
nearer and louder, and they knew that the storm, with
tempest and downpouring and fracas of tossing boughs,
was sweeping toward them over the woods and fields.
The lightning shot through fringes of the coming rain,
and shone in the large, near, slant-streaking drops.

Winslow turned up the collar of his duster, or waterproof, and pulled the flaps over his exposed knees.
Quint likewise turned up his coat-collar and buttoned
the top button, remarking coolly:

"When this tree gets wet through, we can move under
another."

The pleasantry did not appeal to Winslow's sense of
humor. He sprang to his feet with an outburst of
unquotable adjectives, threw down his head against the
gusts, and, exclaiming, "I 'm going to get out of this!"
started to run.

Quint started at the same time, catching him by the
arm.   ·

"Hands off!" Winslow yelled, in the turmoil of rain

and wind and thrashing boughs. "Don't you stop me,
or I 'll—"

"I won't stop you; I 'm going with you," Quint called
back.

"Take that—on your gambrel-roof nose!"—with which
half-stifled ejaculation Winslow whirled and aimed a
furious blow at Quint's head.

Quint ducked in time to receive only a glancing stroke
on his crown. Then, throwing up an elbow to parry a
second blow, he made a headlong dive at Winslow's waist.
He closed with him, and in a moment the two were
engaged in a desperate struggle.

They were about equally matched as to weight, but the
lank Biddicut boy was the taller and longer-limbed of
the two. He had had some school-boy practice at scuf-
fling and wrestling, and his mates had usually found him
what they termed a "tough customer" in their rough-and-
tumble contests. If one attempted to lift him from the
ground, his feet seemed to stick to it as if they had glue
on them, and his sinewy legs to stretch out like legs of
india-rubber.

He gripped Winslow firmly about the waist, at first
with the sole idea of holding him and of shielding his own
head and face from the blows. With his right arm he
managed to secure his favorite under-hold, while his left
fought, and finally grappled, Winslow's right.

Though slight of build, Winslow was lithe and athletic,
and a more formidable adversary than he appeared.
Forced to desist from his blows, he cried, in a lull of the
scuffle:

"Will you let go now?"

"I will," Quint replied, "if you will keep your fists at home."

"And go your way, while I go mine?"

"Your way will be mine till you give me my money!"

"I'll give you a broken back over that log!" Winslow snarled; and the struggle recommenced, both settling down to business.

They tugged and wrenched and lifted, Winslow trying to throw Quint over the log; Quint avoiding it, and at the same time doing his utmost to get Winslow on his hip, fling him, and fall upon him.

Suddenly Winslow, freeing one hand, got it inside his waterproof and into his trousers-pocket. But before he could fairly grasp the knife he was evidently reaching for, his arm was clutched again; he was forced violently backward. In another moment he was himself tripped over the log, and, falling, both went down together.

XXV

A COMPANION FINDS CLIFF

HROUGH all the tumult of the storm Cliff slumbered on his heap of straw, to be at last awakened by something like a blow grazing his cheek and striking him full upon the breast. He started from his dreams, and put out his hand. He thought he was in his bed at home, and that he had been hit by his brother Amos tumbling about in his sleep.

Then it seemed as if something was moving in the room. He heard a rustling sound, and the hand he put out for his brother touched straw.

It was not so dark but that he could see the great open front of the shed, the overhanging roof, and the dim shape of the farm-wagon under it. Recollection returned with a shock, and he was terrified to find that he had fallen asleep while waiting for his friend—he could n't imagine how long ago; it might have been hours.

"Hello!" he cried out, in the wild hope that the movements he had heard were those of Quint, who had perhaps returned to the shed.

No answer. But the movements continued. There was some live creature close behind him; the straw rustled at his very side. He started up, thrilled through and through with horrid fear.

Suddenly the blow on his breast was repeated, and a dark object came between him and the light. Something wet touched his hands; something warm and moist flashed, so to speak, across his face.

His companion in the shed was a dog. The wagging tail thumped his arm; the caressing tongue lapped his face. He uttered a sudden cry—something between a gasp of astonishment and a sob of wildest joy.

"Sparkler! Oh, my gracious Jehu! Sparkler! Quint! Quint!" he called; "I've got him!"—as if Quint were near.

Securing a hold of the collar, he hugged the wet creature to his breast.

"You don't get away from me again, you rogue!" he cried, in a tremor of excitement, as he pulled from his pocket the cord he had carried all day, slipped one end of it about the dog's collar, and fastened it with a firm knot. "Now this never goes out of my hand!"

Sparkler did not even try to get away; he seemed, on the contrary, to recognize Cliff with a pleasure to which his smiting tail gave vivacious expression.

"Why did you run away from me? Why did you come back? How did you find me here?" said the boy, talking as if his dumb companion could comprehend. "Oh, Sparkler, I wish you could speak! What a story you could tell!"

The exciting occurrence diverted his mind for a minute from its anxieties about Quint. But now he thought of him again, with growing amazement and alarm at his mysterious absence. He stilled the dog's movements, and knelt upon the straw, listening and wondering, then advanced to the opening of the shed.

The storm was over; the few drops that fell upon his hand and shoulder came from the still dripping eaves. He went out upon the wet roadside, the dog capering at the end of his cord, and gazed up and down.

"I know something has happened to him!" he wailed, his mind full of torturing conjectures.

The night was not dark, and it seemed to be growing lighter every moment; and he reasoned that it could n't be very late, as there was a glimmer still visible in the windows of the farm-house behind the shed.

He blamed himself bitterly for falling asleep; for it now occurred to him that Quint might have returned to the shed, and, failing to find him in the dark, have gone off in search of him on the lower branch of the forked road.

Or he might have taken refuge in the farm-house close by. But that would n't be like Quint. No; Cliff felt sure that some dreadful thing had befallen his friend.

"Oh, Sparkler," he exclaimed in his misery, "can't you tell me what to do?"

The dog had at first seemed averse to quitting the dark corner of the shed, even bounding back toward the manger when Cliff pulled him away. But now, on the open road, as if he had understood the boy's appeal, he began to tug at the cord in the direction in which Cliff was himself inclined to go.

He hesitated, considering whether he ought not first to make inquiries at the farm-house. As he paused, Sparkler turned and regarded him.

"What is it, Sparkler?" he asked.

The dog leaped up, gave an intelligent bark, and immediately drew the cord again in the direction of the hill road.

"Go ahead!" cried Cliff, with sudden hope and confidence. "I'll trust you!"

He was still full of imaginary fears, but he was comforted by the companionship of the dog, and occasionally, through all his troubles, would break a gleam of pure joy at the thought of Sparkler once more in his possession.

"Won't Quint be glad when he knows!" he said to himself, more than once. "And won't it be strange good luck if it turns out that he has found Winslow, while I have got the dog!"

The hope that this might be so had been among his many conjectures, but he had put it aside as something far too good to be true; it seemed so much more likely that Quint had come to grief in some encounter with the dog-seller.

But Sparkler's actions inspired him; at the same time

10

the world was growing lighter and still lighter, and he perceived that the western sky was clearing. A bright star appeared beneath the edge of broken and low-hanging clouds, and shone with inexpressible beauty and purity in the opening rift. That glimpse of the serene heavens after the storm was like a promise of triumph to the boy's troubled soul.

The rift widened rapidly, showing more and more stars; then all at once a flood of white radiance filled the night. Cliff looked up, and there, almost overhead in the wild sky, was the moon. It peered over the edge of a great black rampart of cloud, as if to reassure the storm-buffeted sphere with its cold, placid smile.

Cliff kept on, often pausing and taxing every sense to discern signs of his lost comrade, until suddenly Sparkler jumped up on the roadside, jerking at the cord. They were on the outskirts of a wood-lot, and a passing gust of wind shook down pattering drops from the branches overhead. The moonlight, slanting through the boughs and silvering the undergrowth, showed a dark log on the ground, toward which Sparkler led the way.

Near the log was a dark-gray object, at which Sparkler was presently sniffing. Cliff ran to it, stooped over it, caught it up, and examined it with astonishment which quickly became consternation. It was a hat.

A common felt hat, of a well-worn appearance, with a narrow brim and shapeless crown, crushed as if it had been trampled on, yet just such a hat as his friend had worn; and there, as if more certainly to identify it, was

"IT WAS A HAT."

a spray of wild roses such as Quint had stuck under the band that afternoon.

Cliff's fears were thus confirmed. Quint had certainly had an encounter with the desperate character they were pursuing, and that he had not had the best of it seemed proved by the fact that his hat, and not Winslow's, was left on the field.

That the wearer himself had not been left with the hat afforded some ground for hope.

"His hat may have been knocked off, and he may have left it to hold on to the fellow," was Cliff's reasonable conjecture. "That would be just like Quint."

But what had happened to him since? In continuing the struggle he might have met with some terrible mishap; and Cliff's excited imagination pictured his friend lying on the ground somewhere in the woods, disabled— possibly worse.

He stood on the edge of the moon-lit woodland, and called with all his force of throat and lungs:

"Hello-o-o, Quint! Hello-o-o!"

His voice died away in the depths of the forest, and not even an echo came back. A curdling terror crept through his veins.

Sparkler meanwhile tugged at his leash and sniffed along the ground. The drenching shower must have carried away, for the most part, such evidences of his master's presence as his delicate canine scent would otherwise have been quick to detect and follow; but he was strangely perturbed.

"Oh, Sparkler!" Cliff pleaded, "seek—seek him!"—in the fond belief that by pursuing Winslow the dog might help him find his friend.

Sparkler's nose stopped at something half buried in a clump of moss. It was a bright object, with a shining edge turned up in the moonlight. Cliff darted to pick it up.

"Only a piece of knife-handle!" he exclaimed. "Have they been breaking knives?" he wondered. It appeared to have been trodden into the moss.

He would have thrown it away as something worthless but for the possibility of its affording some clue to the harrowing mystery.

It was about the size and shape of the thing he took it for, but unlike any knife he had ever seen in Quint's hands. He was carefully scrutinizing it, holding it up in the moonlight with one hand, the end of the cord in the other, along with Quint's hat, wholly forgetting Sparkler in that moment of intense thought, when he was reminded of the dog in an unpleasantly surprising manner.

Sparkler, who had been sniffing again about his feet, gave a sudden bounce; the cord was jerked from Cliff's relaxed hold, and in an instant the dog darted away in the checkered moonshine, with the cord flying like a faint streak at his heels.

"He's gone!" said Cliff, in rage and despair. "Let him go! I wish I had never seen him!"

XXVI

QUINT'S hat had been knocked off by the first glancing blow from Winslow's fist, and when, in the final struggle, they plunged over the log together, the boy from Biddicut struck his unprotected head against the root of a tree. Though partially stunned, he was on his feet again almost immediately, but only in time to see a dim figure dart away, in the rain, in the direction of the cross-road.

Without waiting to recover his hat, or to search for the knife which he thought flew from Winslow's pocket with the outjerked hand, he started at once in pursuit, stumblingly at first, then with more certain steps as he rallied from the effect of his fall.

It was a strange race in the midst of the mad storm, gusts of wind, rain that came down in veiling sheets, lightning-gleams and crashes of thunder. A flash at a critical instant showed the fugitive taking the southern branch of the cross-road, and from that time Quint had little difficulty in following him.

165

At first the distance between them seemed to increase, then for a while to continue about the same. Each had started out with breath spent by the scuffle, and Quint was put to a still further disadvantage by his dive against the tree. Then gradually his forces returned; he drew deep breaths as he ran; and with the sense of restored power the fury of his resolution came back.

So, though a fair match for him in a wrestling-bout, the dog-seller soon found that he could n't compete with the tall Biddicut boy in a foot-race. His breath was utterly gone when, hearing Quint close at his heels, he turned and faced him.

"Are n't we a couple of fools ! " he articulated pantingly.

"If you are speaking for yourself, I don't know of anybody that will dispute you," Quint replied, in much better breath and voice.

He did n't offer to lay hands on Winslow, but, bareheaded, his hair disordered, his features dripping in the rain, and showing a ghastly streak on the left temple, he confronted him.

"What do you propose to do now?" said the dog-seller.

"Stick by you," said Quint, grimly.

"Had n't you better go back and pick up your hat? You seem to have come off in a hurry," said Winslow, his jeering spirit returning.

His own duster, or waterproof, had been torn open in the scuffle, and he was holding it together over his breast.

"If I had known you could n't run any better, I should

have had more leisure," Quint replied. "I might have picked up my hat, and your knife too."

Winslow clapped a hand on his pocket, with a startled look.

"My knife is here," he said. "What are you talking about ?"

"If it 's there, I hope it will keep there," said Quint, with a high and stern expression. "Try to draw it on me again, and I 'll wring your neck as I would a spring chicken's."

"Draw it on you ?" cried the dog-seller. "You 're crazy ! "

"Maybe I did n't keep you busy enough in that little tussle, and you were going to fill up the time whittling the log some more," Quint drawled sarcastically.

"Maybe that, or maybe I thought I could lick a boy like you with one hand in my pocket—as I could, if I had n't stumbled," said Winslow.

"Then what was your terrific hurry to get away—from a boy like me ?" replied Quint.

"To get out of the rain; that 's what I am going to do now," said Winslow, walking on. "Are n't you going back for your hat ?"

"I 've more important business just now," Quint answered, again keeping close to his side.

How extremely anxious he was to go back, he was careful not to betray. Not for his hat, indeed, but in following Winslow he was going farther and farther away from Cliff, of whose assistance he was in such desperate need.

But he would not go back without his captive, nor could he devise any means of taking his captive with him.

It was a singular dilemma—the captive leading away the captor! But there seemed to be no help for it, unless the captor abandoned his purpose, as he had never a thought of doing, although far more apprehensive than he appeared as to the outcome of the amazing adventure.

Winslow would no doubt have offered more liberal terms of settlement if he had known what sort of boy was behind the "gambrel-roof nose." But a rogue may have pride as well as an honest man, and he was not one to give up his ill-gotten "profits" at the demand of a seventeen-year-old "country bumpkin." He knew no more than Quint did how the affair was to end, but he would trust to luck and his good wit to carry him through.

While Quint was bent on sticking to him, he was watching for an opportunity to get rid of Quint. The thunder and lightning ceased, or became distant, but it rained steadily, and the darkness was increasing.

The road ran at right angles from the one to which Quint would gladly have returned; but he shrewdly guessed that it would soon strike one parallel to that, perhaps the main thoroughfare that traversed the village where he had bought crackers and cheese with Cliff, and helped the teamsters with their hot box.

The two walked on without speaking, and before many minutes came to the very street of Quint's conjecture. The cross-road ended there, and a broader highway stretched away in the darkness to the right and left. To

the right it led into an unknown region; to the left it led
back to the village Quint knew.   There were no lights
visible, except in the windows of a few scattered houses.

"Here 's a lamp-post," said Winslow, stopping on a
corner.   "Why is there no light?"

"Because there is supposed to be a moon," replied
Quint.   "That 's the way it is in Biddicut; no matter
how dark and stormy the nights are, the street-lamps
are never lighted. if there happens to be a moon in the
almanac."

"Do you know where we are?" Winslow inquired.

"We are about a mile and a half from the Star Grove
Hotel, which lies in this direction," Quint answered,
pointing.

"That' s according to my calculation," Winslow remarked, as he turned the corner in the direction of the
village, to the immense but secret satisfaction of his
captor.

Another long silence.   They were rapidly approaching
the village.

"Are we going to keep this up all night?" the dog-
seller inquired.

"That 's for you to say," Quint replied.   "If you walk,
I walk.   After the shower is over, exercise will dry us."

Another silence.   Then Winslow asked:

"Where 's Cassius all this time?"

"He 's getting rested, so he 'll be fresh for hooking on
to you, if I find the thing growing monotonous."

"Well," said Winslow, decisively, "I 'm going to the

Star Grove Hotel!"—the lights of which were now visible over the village roofs and trees. "I've engaged a room there."

"I'm with you," Quint remarked cheerfully. "The hotel will be a good place to call a convention of the people you've sold your dog to."

"That's what you propose, is it?" Winslow retorted.

"I don't propose anything. What I do will depend on you. I've only one plan—to get my money back, or to see you locked up. That's the kind of country bumpkin I am."

"You want to try that game?" cried Winslow, defiantly. "Here's your chance!"

It was a chance Quint had been eagerly looking for, with but little hope, however, that he would be allowed to take advantage of it.

They had reached the center of the village, which he recognized, although its aspect was changed from what it had been when he and Cliff passed and repassed through its principal streets that afternoon. They were now plashy and deserted, and doors were closed against the storm. A little off from the corner, not far ahead, was the broadly lighted front window of the grocery on the steps of which Cliff had rested, and munched his crackers and cheese, while Quint went to join the teamsters around the hot box.

On another corner, still nearer, was an establishment in which Quint was more intensely interested just now. This was the police headquarters. Here he had stopped

"'POLICE,' HE CRIED, 'I'VE BROUGHT YOU A HIGHWAY ROBBER!'"

with Cliff to make inquiries, while following Sparkler
back through the village, and had told enough of their
story to insure him a ready hearing, he believed, if he
could now succeed in taking Winslow to the door.

He had hardly expected to bring him even within sight
of it, for Winslow probably knew the town as well as he
did, and that was one of the places which persons of his
character are usually solicitous to avoid.   Perhaps he had
not been so quick as Quint was to recognize the situation;
but he certainly recognized it now. For there, right
across the way, on a broad transparency lighted from
within, were the conspicuous letters—POLICE.

Winslow perceived the sign as soon as Quint did; but
instead of retreating or hurrying by, he put on a bold
front, and repeated:

"Here 's your chance!   Think I 'm afraid of that?"

Fearing some trick, but prepared to fling himself upon
Winslow the instant he should detect an attempt at one,
Quint answered promptly:

"All right! Cross over with me!"

"I 'll do that," said Winslow, "and we 'll soon see
what your blackmailing scheme is good for."

So saying, he crossed over with Quint to the door of
the station.   It was closed, but the light from the window
shone mistily upon them as they stood there a moment
in the rain, alert, suspicious, each eager to fathom the
other's intentions.

"Why don't you go ahead?" said Winslow, with an
ironic smile.

"The oldest first—age before beauty," Quint replied.

"Come along, then!" said the dog-seller, with an air of bravado, mounting the two steps that led to the door.

Quint was so intent upon getting him into the station, and cutting off his retreat in case he should turn back at the last moment, that he was wholly unprepared for what followed.

"Come along!" Winslow repeated, raising his voice as he threw open the door, at the same time clutching the astonished Biddicut boy by the collar and dragging him forward over the threshold. "Police," he cried, "I've brought you a highway robber!"

Captor and captive had all at once changed places.

XXVII

HOW WINSLOW HUNTED FOR HIS WATCH

HERE was but one person in the room, a sturdy Americanized Irishman. Unfortunately, he was not the officer of whom the boys had made inquiries that afternoon. He was writing at a desk in a little railed-off space, with his broad back to the door, when it was burst open in this extraordinary manner.

He stepped promptly outside the rail, and seized hold of Quint, who was struggling with Winslow.

"Be quiet, will you!" Then, to the pretended captor: "What has he done?"

"Stopped me on the street," Winslow exclaimed, showing his thin outer garment torn open at the breast, "snatched my watch, and ran! I caught him, and he flung it away, a few rods back here."

Quint meanwhile was holding fast to Winslow and trying to speak. His bare head, his drenched hair and

175

garments, his rain-streaked features, showing the effects
of his wearisome all-day tramp and of the present excitement,—rendered ghastly, moreover, by an ugly bruise on
the temple,—all combined to give him the aspect of a
desperate and disreputable character.

"Be quiet, or I 'll quiet you!" said the officer. "Take
away your hand!"

Quint released his hold upon Winslow. "I 'll be
quiet," he said; "only let me tell my story."

"You 'll have time for that," said the officer, quickly
slipping a pair of handcuffs on the astounded prisoner.

"Wait till I pick up my watch; I know just where he
dropped it," said Winslow.

"Keep him! keep him! Don't let him go!" Quint
fairly howled.

But Winslow was already out of the station.

He did not lose time in any pretended watch-hunt, but
skipped lightly around the nearest corner, and took his
darksome way toward the Star Grove Hotel.

He had no present intention, however, of seeking the
hospitality of that popular place of resort, although, but
for his untoward adventure with Quint, he might now
have been snugly ensconced behind those warmly lighted
windows, instead of wandering forlorn in a wet and dis-
mal world.

He hurried along the gloomy street with the inviting
hotel lights shining mistily at the end of the vista, but
with his mind turned steadily from that temptation,
toward some less public place of refuge. A young man

of ready resources, he kept his eye out for opportunities, and discovered one before he had gone far.

A little way back from the street, a stable door stood open, showing a dimly lighted interior, and the silhouette of a horse's hind quarters dark against the glow beyond. Keeping close by the fence, he slipped in at the gate, and, avoiding the faint glimmer of diffused light shed before the doorway, got into the shadow, close against the corner of the stable.

There he paused to consider the situation and learn if his movements had been observed. The rain was about over, but a tin eaves-spout gurgled and tinkled in his ear as he peered cautiously around the door-post.

He could hear the tranquil champing of the horses at their racks, and sounds as of some person scattering the litter of their beds, or slapping one to make him give room. The unbidden guest quietly stepped inside, ready with some word to excuse his presence in case it should be challenged. The nearest horse, whose silhouette he had seen from without, stopped champing, and turned his head to regard the stranger; but the horse in the next stall nippingly pulled a fresh wisp of hay from his rack, and the rustle of the bedding-down continued.

At the left of the entrance was a stairway leading to some dark loft, and beside the stairway was a passage opening into a gloomy space, which he judged rightly to be the barn part of the premises. His choice lay between the passage and the stairway, and choosing the passage, he tiptoed into it.

"Stand around!" ordered the man in the stalls, giving another flank a resounding slap, and a quick movement of hoofs sounded in the stalls.

Winslow grew bolder. Along the range of stalls beneath the loft was an opening in the partition, through which the lantern-light threw broken gleams over the horses' heads and through the racks half filled with hay, enabling the dog-seller to make out the principal objects in what promised to afford a safe and cozy hiding-place.

Before him was a loaded hay-wagon, pretty well filling the front space of the barn. In the rear was a covered carriage, with boxes and barrels dimly discernible in a far corner. The barn was full of the fragrance of new hay, and there was hay scattered on the floor, under the side of the loaded rick.

To creep under the wagon and pull some of this litter over him, or to climb into the carriage and intrench himself in cushions, or even to crouch behind the barrels until he could have a little time to consider—he had his choice of these expedients. But he adopted neither. Seeing a ladder placed against the broad bulk of the load, he mounted it nimbly, and laid himself flat on the hay.

He soon heard the man in the stalls go out, speaking to the horses as he passed their heels, and closing the door after him. With the man went the lantern, and the barn was left in darkness and in silence, except that the horses continued to champ, and now and then one changed his footing on the plank floor.

Winslow now sat up, and, removing his torn water-

proof, spread it on the hay.   He cared for his hat (origi-
nally of stiff straw) by placing it on a smooth part of the
garment, with the rim downward, to preserve its shape in
drying.   He had more trouble with his soaked boots, but
he got them off too, after some panting efforts.

He was quite self-possessed, and no doubt congratu-
lated himself on his good luck.   If he had any fear that
he might have been seen entering the stable, it passed
quickly.

"I seem to be right side up with care!" he said to
himself, as he loosened his damp and matted locks, and
buried his feet in the dry hay.   "Wonder how it is with
friend Marcus Brutus!"

If he had been vastly worse off than he found himself,
he would have had to laugh at the neat trick he had
played upon that "country bumpkin."

He was certain he had heard a lock click, after the man
with the lantern went out and shut the door.   But that
did n't give him the least concern.   He had no doubt of
being able to open some other door from the inside, or at
least a window, and effect an easy and safe egress sometime in the still hours of the early morning.   It was n't
like being in the lockup!

"I prefer to furnish a substitute for that," he chuckled.
"This is n't a first-class hotel,—not the Star Grove,—but
it will do for Algernon K. W., under existing circumstances."

The barn did n't seem very dark after his eyes got
accustomed to the obscurity, and before long the win-

11

dows, of which he had two in sight as he sat up, brightened with signs of a clearing sky. It was still early in
the evening, he was habituated to late hours, and his nap
in the Star Grove hammock left him little disposed to
sleep.

Rest and warmth and a sense of security were agreeable to him, however, and, stretching himself out on the
hay, he occupied a wakeful hour in planning further
operations with Sparkler.

A shaft of moonlight slanted through one of the
sashes, and filled the gloomy solitude with a soft translu-
cency. The horses ceased champing, and soon one of
them lay down in the stall with a comfortable groan. It
was time for the adventurer to get a little sleep, in order
to make his contemplated early start in the morning.
He was just falling into a drowse when he was startled
out of it by the opening of a door, the sound of voices,
and the shining of a lantern in the barn.

XXVIII

EVEN with the handcuffs on his wrists, Quint would have rushed out in pursuit of the escaping Algernon, if the officer had n't detained him.

"*He* is the robber! Let me go!" he cried, trying to get away.

"Will you quit?" demanded the officer, holding him firmly by one manacled wrist.

"I 'll quit if I must," Quint replied; "but I never thought it was the business of the police to help the rogues instead of the honest men."

"We 'll see who is the rogue in this case," said the officer, slightly disconcerted by Winslow's sudden disappearance, and by the prisoner's vehement protest— "when he comes back with the watch."

"There was no watch!" Quint declared. "He won't come back! If he does, you may believe I am the robber, and not that *he* has got *my* money."

It is not probable that the deliberative Biddicut boy

181

had ever before spoken so volubly and vehemently. Fully roused, furiously indignant, he turned from gazing after the vanished figure, and glared upon the officer.

Only the rain was heard outside the open door. The sound of fleeing footsteps had died away. No figure groping along the ground in search of a watch, nor any other moving object, was visible in the plashy street. After looking out and listening a moment, the officer addressed his prisoner:

"What were you resisting for?"

"I was n't resisting; I was only trying to hold on to him, while you were letting him go. Could n't you see what he was up to?" said Quint, his grim face wrathfully glowering. "*I* had brought *him* in, instead of his bringing me!"

"It did n't look so," said the officer, incredulous, but evidently disturbed. "He was dragging you after him."

"I 'll tell you how that was," said Quint. "The minute I got him to the door, and was making him come in first, he grabbed me by the collar and snaked me over the top step so suddenly I stumbled. Then you thought I was fighting to get away, when I was only keeping *him* from getting away."

The officer was all the while looking out for the returning watch-hunter and frowning dubiously. Again he turned and looked Quint carefully over.

"It 's an improbable story you tell," he declared. "You could n't capture and bring in a man like him. Impossible!"

"Would it be any more possible for him to bring me in?" Quint retorted, standing at his full height, and looking sternly into the eyes of the officer, who, though a good-sized man, was hardly taller than he.

"You are bigger than I thought when you came sprawling in."

"You thought then I was big enough to play the highway robber. I own I could n't have brought him here if he had n't been willing, any more than he could have brought me. I had been following him all day—I had just caught him—and then to have the *police* help him get away!"

Quint crushed some angry word in his teeth, and his ghastly features worked with repressed emotion.

"How had *he* robbed *you?*" the officer demanded.

Quint told something of the dog-seller's operations, and went on :

"We followed him all the way from Biddicut, through I don't know how many towns. I was alone when I fell in with him this evening. He tried to shake me off, and we had a squabble. But I stuck to him till we came in sight of your station. Then I should have called for help, if he had n't himself proposed to come in. He had his trick already planned."

"Did he give you that blow on the forehead?" the officer inquired.

Quint put up his hand. "I did n't know I had one! He struck me three or four times. But I must have got this when we fell over a log together, and my head tried to occupy the same place with the butt of a tree," he explained solemnly.

The officer, evidently no longer expectant of Winslow, kept glancing up at the clock. He had told Quint he could sit down, but Quint remained standing.

"The chief will be here in a few minutes," the man said. "Then, if we find you are telling a straight story, we'll see what we can do for you."

"You can't do anything now," Quint answered sullenly, "unless you take off these bracelets. They are n't comfortable, and they are n't ornamental, and they happen to be on the wrong pair of wrists. The other pair is far enough out of your reach by this time. After all the trouble we'd had!" He choked a little. "Nobody is going to follow him again as we followed him!"

Footsteps were heard approaching along the wooden sidewalk. They were heavier than the tread of the light-heeled young dog-seller. Another officer stepped up on the threshold, handling a furled umbrella. Quint recognized him as the one he and Cliff had made inquiries of that afternoon, but said nothing.

The newcomer regarded the Biddicut boy with astonishment, recognizing him only after an effort of puzzled reflection.

"Hello!" he said, "what has happened to you?"

"Ask him!" Quint replied, with morose wrath.

"What is it, Terry?" the chief demanded.

Terry told his story. Then Quint told all that was necessary of his. An expression of disgust settled upon the face of the chief—a much more refined and intelligent face than that of the subordinate.

"Terry," he said, "it 's a prodigious blunder. This boy's story corresponds with what he and his chum told me this afternoon. That fellow won't find any watch; 't is n't a good night for finding watches. Take off that pair of rings!"

Terry quietly removed the handcuffs.

"Now, go out and see if you can find anything of the other party to this affair," said his superior. "I 'll give you fifteen minutes to produce him, with or without the watch. If he does n't put in an appearance by that time, we shall know he 's a fraud."

.With a sarcastic smile he watched Terry's departure on his ridiculous errand, then looked at Quint, silent, surly, his pale face rain-streaked and blood-stained, his wet clothes beginning to steam in the warm air of the station.

"You may as well sit down and take it easy," the chief said kindly, pushing a stool toward him.

"I 'm too mad to sit down," said Quint. "Besides, my partner is waiting for me in that cart-shed, if he is n't hunting for me. I must put out and find him, as soon as you make up your minds that I 'm not a highwayman."

He seated himself on the stool, nevertheless, with a strangely haggard aspect.

"You 've had a pretty hard time," observed the chief, regarding him curiously.

"I have n't had leisure to think of that," Quint replied. "If I had kept the fellow, that would have rested me for

all my life! I should n't mind anything—lost hat, empty
stomach, broken head, wet skin! As it is—" He choked
up again with rage and grief.

"I 'll dry you off," said the chief, stooping to open the
door of an air-tight stove.

There were kindlings laid in it, ready for lighting. He
touched a match to them, and in a few seconds it was
roaring and cracking close behind the boy's wet back.

"I wish—Cliff—was here," Quint murmured, with a
long-drawn sigh. Even he was breaking down at last.

Considerably within the allotted fifteen minutes Terry
returned, disconsolate, and obliged to confess that his
watch-hunter was still missing.

"But he looked so respectable, compared with — " he
glanced at poor Quint on his stool—"anybody might
have made the mistake."

"Anyhow, it has been made," said the chief, "and now
we must see what can be done to rectify it. We can't
catch the scamp,—not to-night, anyway,—but we may do
something for this boy. It 's time to be thinking of that."

It was time indeed. His weariness and discouragement, the reaction from his late terrible excitement, his
want of substantial food, and now the stifling heat of the
stove and the odor of his own steaming garments, were
producing an alarming effect upon the boy from Biddicut. He turned sick and dizzy, and the chief had but
just time to spring to his support when he reeled sidewise, tumbling from the stool.

XXIX

WHAT WAS HIDDEN IN THE MANGER

HE last trick of the trick-dog had surprised Cliff at a moment when he was so full of trouble that he exclaimed, in his despair, "Let him go!" and cared little if he never beheld him again. What disappointments, what fatigues, that wily and treacherous animal had caused him! And now had come this climax of the boy's woes, this horrible uncertainty as to what had befallen his faithful friend Quint.

He would scarcely have gone out of his way to resume his pursuit of the fugitive; nevertheless, even in his wretched state of mind, it was a matter of interest that Sparkler had gone back in the direction from which they had come—the way Cliff must himself now return.

He called again; he explored the ground all about—under the trees, and in the corners of the intersecting roads. He looked off in every direction, in the vain hope of seeing a human figure start out, somewhere, from

187

amidst the shadows; then, with a heavy heart, he turned back toward the roadside shed.

He had but a flickering hope of finding that Quint had reached the rendezvous, and it died within him before he had fairly passed beneath the shadow cast by the roof upon the moon-lit wayside. He called Quint's name, and kicked the heap of straw; for although his friend was foremost in his thoughts, he also entertained the possibility of Sparkler's having sought again that comfortable bed. But neither dog nor friend made sound or sign in that solitary shelter.

One thing remained now to do—to go to the farmhouse where he had seen a light, make known his distress, and ask for advice, if not for assistance. He wished he had done so before; he wished so with bitter regret when, looking again, he saw that the light was extinguished.

He stood gazing at the darkened windows, and up and down the road, when he perceived another light. It was not in any farm-house; it was evidently in motion; it was approaching in the middle of the highway. The moonbeams reduced its rays to a feeble glimmer, and soon revealed the form of a man carrying it—a stocky man, in a buttoned frock-coat, and wearing a round-topped hat.

Cliff watched his approach, and drew back into the shed to wait, filled with a fearful hope that the coming of the man with the lantern somehow concerned him and Quint and their strange night adventure.

"If he is coming for me, he will stop here," he said to himself. "If he is going by, I will stop him." And he waited in breathless suspense.

Arrived at the shed, the man turned into it, and, holding up the lantern where Cliff stood in the shadow, cast its light upon both their faces. His own was that of a ruddy Americanized Irishman—our friend Terry's, in short.

"Are you the boy from Biddicut?" he inquired, peering at Cliff curiously.

Cliff had already noticed, with a thrill of surprise, that the stocky man wore the uniform of a police officer.

"The other Biddicut boy sent you?" he answered eagerly. "Where is he?"

"Down at the police station," the officer replied; "and I have come to fetch you."

"Arrested?" Cliff gasped out, with a face of wonder and fear.

"Not exactly," said the man; "but he has had a rough time. He was troubled about you, and I offered to come and find you."

He would have hit the truth nearer the bull's-eye if he had said that he came at the suggestion of his superior officer, and by way of partial atonement for the blunder of which poor Quint had been made the victim.

Cliff anxiously inquired what had happened to the other boy from Biddicut.

"Nothing very serious," said Terry. "Only he caught your dog-dealer, and had a set-to with him."

"That 's what I was afraid of!" Cliff exclaimed. "He got hurt?"

"He came in for a little punishment," said Terry. "But he stuck to him, and brought him to the station."

"Oh, Quint! He 's great!" cried Cliff, with premature exultation.

"'T was a fine piece of work," Terry admitted; "but at the last moment the rogue turned the tables on him by a cunning trick, and got away."

"Oh! how could he?" Cliff wailed.

"I'll tell you on the way back. We 've made your friend pretty comfortable, and he wants you to join him. That 's his hat you have? I was to look for that as well as for you."

"To think," exclaimed Cliff, "that he should have caught Winslow, and I the dog, and that both should have got away!"

He was explaining how Sparkler had found him on the straw there, when he paused in amazement at sight of an object revealed by the rays of Terry's lantern. It was a piece of most familiar-looking cord hanging over the side of the manger.

He sprang to seize hold of it.

"The lantern! hold the lantern!" he cried, slipping his hand swiftly along the cord toward some object to which it was evidently attached.

Terry lifted the lantern, and exposed to view, curled up in the bottom of the manger, and pretending to be fast asleep, but doubtless as wide awake as any four-footed creature on the face of the globe at that moment, the

"'I'LL HOLD YOU THIS TIME, IF I LIVE!' CLIFF EXCLAIMED JUBILANTLY"

twice-lost Sparkler!—Sparkler, wisest of dogs, yet not wise enough to consider that it was a short-sighted and ostrich-like policy, in hiding, to leave the end of his leash trailing so far behind him!

"I 'll hold you this time, if I live!" Cliff exclaimed jubilantly.

He examined the loop he had previously knotted about the collar, and made sure that the dog had not attempted to gnaw the cord, the other end of which he now tightened in a slip-noose about his own wrist.

"I ought to have done this before," he said; "but I had what I thought was a good turn of it around my hand, when he jumped so suddenly and snatched it away from me.   What do you mean, Sparkler?"

Sparkler stood with his fore paws on the side of the manger, wagging his tail, and looking brightly conscious, as his custom was, after the performance of a successful trick.   He seemed not at all averse to being recaptured by the boy who had lately been his master; he even showed his teeth with something like a laugh.

"I declare, he 's grinning at me!" Cliff exclaimed.   "I can't make him out.   I thought he ran in here in the first place to get out of the rain; and he seemed so pleased to have found me, I was quite taken in and thrown off my guard.   He sha'n't fool me so again."

Sparkler wagged and winked, and kept his expressive mouth open just enough to hint his appreciation of the joke.   He seemed reluctant to leave the manger, but Cliff forced him to take the leap.

"What 's this, do you believe? He was guarding something," said Terry, lowering his lantern into the vacated manger.

Sparkler sprang back instantly, the length of his leash, and seizing the officer's coat-tail, tugged at it with a menacing snarl.

"Sparkler, behave!" Cliff commanded, pulling him off. "See what it is; I 'll hold him."

Terry thereupon fished up a curiously shaped roll, which fell open in his hand and assumed the shape of a flat, empty bag, Sparkler growling and springing to get at him.

"That 's Winslow's!" cried Cliff, in high excitement. "It 's his gray linen gripsack! I understand the business now!"

As the officer was mystified, the boy briefly explained:

"He followed Winslow as long as Winslow carried that. It might be a roll he could put into his pocket, or it might be a bag with his duster in it. But if he left it anywhere, then the dog knew he was to meet him at that place, or wait for him there, after they had separated. He had come back to stay with the bag when he found me here."

"If that was the scheme," observed Terry, "then your man will be coming around sometime to meet your dog."

"That 's so!" said Cliff. "He might have been on his way here when Quint tackled him—though the dog could hardly have been expected to get back here so soon. When he is sold in the evening, I don't suppose he usually gets away before morning. That was my experience with him. What shall we do with the bag?"

"Leave it just as we found it," said Terry. "The owner will be coming for it in the morning, and to keep his appointment with the dog, unless he is shadowing us now, which I don't think likely."

"It must have been covered with straw; I got all of this litter out of the manger," said Cliff. "That may have been what upset the dog's calculations—to find me here, lying on the straw that should have been in the manger with the bag under it. Now let's have it all back, and put out the light, and leave everything till my partner and I can come in the morning and waylay Winslow."

XXX

WHAT CLIFF CARRIED IN HIS POCKET

PARKLER had become quiet after the bag was returned to its place, and he followed readily when Cliff led him from the shed, and set off, guided by Terry, down the moon-lit road.

"What time is it?" Cliff inquired.

The officer pulled out his watch, and turned its white countenance up to the moon.

"Twenty minutes of nine."

"No later!" exclaimed Cliff. "Will any stores be open in the village?"

"They keep open till nine, as a general thing. If we step along lively we may get there before they close. Do you want to patronize them to-night?"

"There's one thing I must have."

"Before you go to the station and see your friend?"

"Yes, even before that; for after that it might be too late."

Cliff explained his purpose, and, on entering the village,

Terry took him to a store where small articles of hardware were retailed. He laid Quint's hat on the counter, and inquired:

"Have you a small chain for my dog, in place of this cord?"

The storekeeper showed his wares; but the smallest chain would have served better for hitching horses than for leading a fastidious dog like Sparkler. The boy looked disappointed, but, brightening presently, asked:

"Have you any copper wire?"

Some samples being shown him, he selected one that was sufficiently light and flexible, and said: "Cut me off three yards of this."

The piece obtained, he made one end fast to the dog's collar, then passed the rest in a long spiral around the entire cord, including the loop at his wrist. The two men watched him with interest, giving him such assistance as he required; but Sparkler looked sleepy and indifferent.

"He may gnaw the cord, but I defy him to bite off the wire! How much is to pay?"

As he said this he thrust his free hand into his pocket, and drew it out again with something that might have been silver or nickel, but was n't money.

"What's this?" he muttered, and it was a moment before he recognized the shining object he had picked up near the spot where he found Quint's hat. He had not since given it a thought; indeed, he had hardly been conscious of slipping it into his pocket in the moment of surprise when Sparkler got away from him. Examined

12

in the lamplight, it resembled less the part of a knife-handle, which he had at first taken it for. It was in shape a long oval, about three inches in length by nearly three quarters of an inch in width, thin, and slightly curved. In the inner surface were two short rivets. The outer surface was brightly polished, with rounded edges, and it bore an engraved inscription.

Cliff held it up to the light, and read the lettering, with a face betraying the utmost astonishment, his eyes staring from his head, and his lips forming an inaudible exclamation. Then he flung himself upon Sparkler as if with intent to throttle instantaneously that unconcerned and impassive quadruped.

His immediate business, however, was not so much with the dog as with the dog's collar. This, it will be remembered, was a strap of maroon-colored leather, starred with nickel studs about an inch and a half apart, except in one place, where two studs seemed to be missing.

With hands trembling in their eagerness, Cliff applied his metal plate to the space thus left, and found that it not only fitted it, but that the rivets corresponded exactly with the two rivet-holes in the collar.

He sprang to his feet, and was rushing from the store in his excitement, when Terry called after him:

"You 're leaving your friend's hat; shall I bring it?"

"Yes, please!" cried Cliff, hardly knowing what he said.

"Shall I pay for the wire, too?"

Cliff turned back, and held out all his small change in his open palm. Whether the storekeeper took much or little, he was in no state of mind to care.

"You seem to be in a rush, all at once," the man remarked, with a smile.

"Jehu! who would n't be? Excuse me!" said Cliff, remembering that a little politeness would n't be out of place. "Now, where 's my chum?"

And boy and dog disappeared with the officer.

Cliff was unwilling to tell any one of his discovery until he had imparted the tremendous secret to his friend. "What Quint would say" was the thought uppermost in his mind as he accompanied Terry to the station.

The door was wide open, and within sat Quint, with his back to the stove, and his coat and vest hanging near it, over the office railing. On the stove were two bowls containing hot chocolate, and on a stool beside him was a tray pretty well loaded with what looked to be a comfortable repast for two—boiled eggs as white as the saucer that held them, a loaf of bread, butter and salt, knives and spoons and plates. The air of the room was warm, despite the open door, and humid from the vapor of steaming garments.

This banquet set before him must have been tempting to the tired and hungry boy, now quite recovered from his faintness; but Quint was unwilling to taste food until his friend, then momently expected, could partake of it with him.

The appearance of Cliff at the door, with Sparkler

capering before him, very nearly proved disastrous to the contents of the tray, which Quint's knee knocked in his sudden attempt to rise. Fortunately, he caught it, and steadied it on the stool.

"The dog?" he cried, his face lighting up joyfully. "Cliff, you 've beat me! I 'm glad one of us has had some luck!"

"Don't say luck till I tell you!" replied Cliff, in gleeful agitation. "Whether it 's luck or not, I don't know; but it 's great!"

"Why, what 's that?" Quint asked, as Cliff held out to him the metal plate.

"Read what 's on it; then I 'll show you!"

No common adjectives seemed strong enough to express Quint's astonishment as he read the inscription; but the famous words of Brutus, which he had so often spouted, broke from his lips with a force of feeling he had never put into them before:

"'Be ready, gods, with all your thunderbolts!' Where did you come by that?"

"See how it fits?" said Cliff, pulling Sparkler forward, parting his curls, and showing the place in the collar which the plate and the rivets fitted. "I found it near your hat, up there in the woods. Winslow must have lost it."

"And I know just how he lost it," exclaimed Quint.

"May I see it?" asked the chief.

"Yes; you can see it," said Cliff, passing the name-plate over to the chief, who read the inscription with delighted curiosity.

"'*P. T. Barnum*'!" he exclaimed. "'*Bridgeport, Conn. License* 373.' Thunderation, young fellows! That 's Barnum's celebrated circus dog! He 's worth a thousand dollars!"

He passed the plate over to Terry, and looked down with a smile of lively interest on the meek-eyed Sparkler.

Terry likewise read the lettering, slapped his knee in wonder and admiration, and stared enviously at the rather insignificant-looking quadruped, exclaiming:

"There 'll be a big reward offered! I wish I had captured him!"

He returned the metal plate to the chief, who handed it back to Cliff, saying:

"I don't see but that you 've got the inside track, boys! He 'll be worth a deal more to you than he has cost, if he is *that* dog."

Cliff stroked the spaniel's head affectionately.

"If he belongs to Barnum, Barnum must have him back again, I suppose. I only wish he was mine! Now, tell about your scrape with Winslow, Quint."

"You tell first how you found the dog," Quint said.

"Pitch into your supper, boys," counseled the chief, "and tell your stories over your eggs and chocolate."

"That 's judgmatical advice!" observed Quint.

XXXI

HOW THE BOYS FOUND SUPPER AND LODGING

"SUPPER? our supper?" said Cliff, eying the contents of the bowls and tray with an interest which the more exciting question of the moment could not wholly eclipse. "How is that?"

"We sometimes have to feed a prisoner, and your friend here came so near being one that I thought we owed him a treat. He 'll tell you about it, or perhaps Terry would prefer to—eh, Terry? Well, lay to, boys, before the eggs get any colder."

He placed a second chair for Cliff opposite Quint's, with the tray on the stool between them, and handed them the chocolate. Hungry, happy, grateful, they cracked their eggs and told their stories, while Terry, kneeling before the open stove door, toasted slices of bread for them on a fork.

Cliff thought this a most extraordinary service for a police officer to render to a couple of wayfaring boys, but did not conceive that it placed them under very great obligations when he learned, what Terry had not yet told him, how Winslow had been aided to escape.

Quint in his narrative cast no blame upon the officer, but called it a "natural mistake," and took his slice of crisp toast from the friendly hands that prepared it, buttered it and soaked it in his chocolate, and ate it with immense relish, declaring they "would have Winslow yet."

"He will certainly go back to the shed for the dog and his bag," he said, "and we must be there to nab him, very early in the morning, if we don't go to-night. I am getting dry and rested, and I'm not two thirds as hungry as I was before I had my supper. How is it with you, partner?"

"My little nap in the shed was almost as good as a night's sleep," Cliff replied. "Then, there was a good deal of the right kind of medicine in catching the dog, finding you all right—and such a supper as this! I could start for home, if there was any hope of reaching it in three or four hours."

As that was out of the question, the chief offered to find lodgings for them in a house near by, where their supper had been ordered. But Cliff said:

"We have n't money enough for that; I'm afraid it's going to break us, just paying for this picnic."

"That's not going to cost you anything," said the chief; "neither shall a bed in the boarding-house. We're bound to do so much for you."

"You are awfully kind!" said Cliff. "But we can

turn in only for a little while, and I must n't be parted from this dog."

"Then allow me to make a suggestion," said the chief, between puffs of his cigar. "We've got a couple of cells down-stairs, and they open into an airy room, unoccupied—no bedding, straw mattresses, rather thin, but clean. You won't find 'em bad to sleep on, and you can keep the dog with you."

Cliff shrugged, and lifted his eyebrows at Quint. Quint smiled his drollest smile as he poised his nearly empty chocolate-bowl, and looked quizzically at Cliff over the devastated tray.

"It will be enough for me to brag of, that I 've had on a pair of iron wris'bands," he remarked. "If I should let on to the boys in Biddicut that I 'd slept in a police-station, I would n't answer for the result; I 'm afraid some of 'em would die of envy!"

The chief laughed as he knocked the ashes off his cigar, while Terry stood by and grinned.

"If we could get into a barn somewhere, and put in three or four hours' sleep on the hay," said Cliff, "that would be better than going back to the shed before daylight."

"That would suit me," said Quint. "I 've more than once slept in a barn, in summer, just for fun. I 'm getting dry enough."

He put on his vest, but held his coat to the fire for a turn or two, while Cliff offered the fragments of their repast to Sparkler. The dog had declined food at first, and he now winked at it somewhat contemptuously as he lay curled up by the stove.

"If you had spoken about the barn a little earlier, I might have managed it," said Terry. "Deacon Payson's barn," with a consulting glance at the chief. "Maybe I can now. The deacon is usually up later than this."

As the boys welcomed the suggestion, Terry, with the chief's approval, went out to see what arrangements could be made. In his absence the boys talked over their affairs with the chief, and got his advice as to what they should do if they found Winslow, what in case they did n't, and as to their best course in regard to the dog that had in so extraordinary a manner come into their possession.

Then Terry returned, and said: "It 's all right! Deacon Payson's hay-mow will accommodate you."

He relighted his lantern, Quint put on his coat and shoes, and Cliff, with a pull of the wire-wound cord, woke up Sparkler dozing by the stove. Then the boys shook hands with the chief, who wished them luck and promised them further assistance if they should require it, and they departed, preceded by Terry carrying his lantern, and followed by the dispirited spaniel.

A little way up the street, Terry knocked at a door, which was opened by an old gentleman in shirt-sleeves.

"I 've brought my young chaps, Mr. Payson," said the officer, stepping aside, and holding his lantern so that his "young chaps" could be seen.

The old gentleman looked them over, and fixed his eyes on Quint.

"I thought so," he remarked. "I 've seen one of 'em before. Have n't I?"

"You were in the crowd around the hot box this afternoon, when I was inquiring for a man and a dog," Quint replied, glad to recognize the kindly face.

"Terry tells me you want to bunk in my barn," said the old gentleman. "I 'll be with you in a second."

He stepped back into the room, and reappeared, putting on his coat, and holding a key in his teeth. This he shifted to a hand that came through the ample coat-sleeve, and led the way along a path lighted by the mingled rays of the moon and of Terry's lantern. Having unlocked a stable door, he took the lantern from Terry's hand, and preceded the others, past a stall, in which there was a horse lying down, into a well-filled barn beyond.

"Here 's hay right here on the floor," he said; "and I can get you blankets."

"If it was my case," said Terry, "I should get up on this load of hay. Here 's a ladder placed a-purpose. Then you 'll be out of the way of rats."

Quint surveyed the premises with satisfaction, and said he was n't afraid of rats.

"Particularly with the dog to sleep with us," Cliff added, laughing. "He 's good for almost everything else; he ought to be death on rats! I believe he smells 'em now!"

Sparkler was, in fact, sniffing about excitedly, putting his nose in the loose hay, whining, and finally setting his fore feet on a round of the ladder, with a wistful upward look, as if he had understood and approved Terry's suggestion.

"The dog votes for the top of the load," said Quint, "and I 'm not so sure but it will be the best place for us. It may be the safest for him, if he is going to try any more of his tricks."

"You mean, if he gets away from me?" said Cliff. "He is n't going to do that, I tell you! But if he should, he 'd find his way down from that load quicker than you or I could!"

"I guess the best place is right here on the floor," Quint concluded. "'T won't do any harm to pull down a little more hay, will it?"

"None at all," Mr. Payson replied. "And here are some carriage cushions."

"Quint, this is a luxury!" cried Cliff.

"Cliff, this is judgmatical!" replied Quint. "We could n't ask anything better, if we were presidents of these United States!"

"I wish our folks could know!" said Cliff. "How are we to get out in the morning?"

"I shall have to lock you in," Mr. Payson answered. "But if you are stirring before my man comes around, you can open this big front door from the inside; I 'll show you how the swivel-bar works. Or you can unbolt the door in the rear."

"Shall I go up on the load and throw down a little more hay?" Quint said, starting to climb the ladder.

"I can get plenty," said Mr. Payson, bringing a rake, and reaching up with it to the edge of the load. "Now I think you will be all right. Unless you start too early in the morning, my folks can give you some breakfast."

"If you want any help from us, you 'll find the station open," said Terry. "I 'll post the night-officer, so there 'll be no more mistakes at our end of the line."

The boys had made their bed between the end of the load and the front door, and were preparing to lie down in their clothes, after kicking off their shoes.

"Come here, now!" Cliff commanded, making Sparkler lie down by his side. "He heard us talk of rats, and can't forget it." He took the precaution to make a couple of turns with the leash about his arm, in addition to the loop at his wrist. "Even if he should get loose, I don't suppose he can get out of the barn."

"Not before the doors are opened," Mr. Payson replied, regarding his guests with amused satisfaction. "I don't see but what you are pretty cozy."

With an exchange of "good nights," the men went out with the lantern, and the boys found themselves alone on the floor of the great, shadowy, moon-visited barn.

XXXII

A STRANGE FELLOW-LODGER

" DON'T know how to thank folks," said Cliff. "Somehow, when anybody has been good to you, any words about it sound foolish."

"We have had more kindness shown to us than anything else, on this trip," Quint replied, "even with Winslow and the old cook in the opposite scale."

"I 'm thinking," said Cliff, "we 'd better let Winslow slide. Now we 've got the dog, we can't make enough out of him to pay for the trouble."

"I 'm a little surprised at you, Cliff," Quint answered, after a moment's silence. "You hurt my feelings when you speak like that. After we got started on this expedition, and it was growing a little mite interesting, you 'd have given it up two or three times if it had n't been for me."

"I 've wished we had given it up more times than that," Cliff confessed. "Think of what you have gone

through! Such a wetting as you got, and the tumble the
rascal gave you, up there in the woods, let alone his
turning you over to the police! It makes me laugh,
though, to think of that."

"We 'll laugh at the whole thing when we 're safe
through it," said Quint. "Maybe we sha'n't get much
satisfaction out of Algernon, in one way, even if we
catch him. But as I owe him for the wetting, and the
broken head, and the cold wris'bands, not to mention
other small items, I want to pay him in a lump, and get
his receipt in full. In short, I mean to get even with
Algernon K., if it takes another day to do it."

Cliff made no reply to this declaration, which suggested such possibilities of still further hardships and
disappointments. Quint waited a minute, then went on,
in a tone which betrayed how deeply hurt he was by his
friend's silence:

"You 've got the dog, and now you naturally want to
hurry away with him. That 's all right, Cliff. That 's
the important thing to you. The important thing to me
is the bear-hug I am saving up for Winslow. This may
be a weakness on my part, and I 've no doubt the course
you propose is the wisest. But if I don't get in that
squeeze, I shall feel a want, as if I 'd missed something
useful and agreeable, all the rest of my life."

"I feel just so, too," Cliff replied. "Although we 've
got the dog, I never shall feel quite happy about it,
unless we get Winslow. But I 'm doubting whether the
chance of catching him is worth what it will cost." .

"We can only find that out by making the trial. Just give me a little help in the morning," said Quint; "then, if we don't scoop him in, and if I should feel like sticking to his trail a little longer, I 'll go ahead on my own account, and let you start for home without me."

Cliff's free hand reached over and gave Quint's arm an affectionate grip.

"See here, Quint," he said; "don't misunderstand me. Remember what Cassius says: 'A friend should bear a friend's infirmities.' I 've played that part to your Brutus too many times to have a disagreement with you in earnest."

"Oh, it 's no disagreement," Quint protested.

"Fact is," said Cliff, "I got used up too soon in this tramp; I have n't anything of your tremendous stick-to-it-iveness; and I—but no matter!"—choking a little. "You 've been such a friend to me—you 've helped me get the dog, which is your dog now just as much as he is mine; and now I 'm going to help you overhaul Winslow again, no matter how many days it takes; and you won't hear me say another word about turning back, as long as you want to follow him."

"Cliff, you are the pluckiest fellow I ever saw!" Quint exclaimed, and by this time the boys' two hands had clasped in a fervent, mutual pressure. "Pluckier than I am!"

"Don't be absurd!" Cliff remonstrated, with something like tears in his laugh.

"I mean it!" said Quint. "You have stuck to this

business, when you 've seen it would be a good deal wiser to give it up. I am a little more obstinate than you are, that 's all. And now you offer to give up your wisdom to my obstinacy. I think we 've a good chance of trapping Winslow in the morning. We 'll try it, do our level best, and if we don't succeed, then—homeward bound, say I ! "

"You 've found out you can outrun him; that 's a strong point in our favor," said Cliff. "We 'll be cautious, though; we 'll be early in the shed."

"For that reason," Quint replied, "we must stop talking now, and get some sleep. I shall be awake by the time the birds are twittering."

"I forgot you had n't had a nap, as I had," said Cliff. "I feel as if I could talk all night. Is n't it pleasant in here?—the moonlight slanting in at that window and striking down over the stalls! Sparkler is sleeping, as quiet and contented as the most honest dog in the world."

Quint made no reply, and his heavy breathing soon showed that he was asleep; nor was it long before Cliff succumbed to blissful drowsiness, and slept on their bed of hay, between his friend and his dog.

The moonbeams mounted higher and higher, and shot their penciling radiance through the racks, as the great, slow, solemn, starry wheel of night rolled on. The last fading yesterday joined all the countless yesterdays of the past, and another untried morrow was at hand.

Then a dark figure crept over the edge of the high load of hay, put one foot after the other on the rounds of the

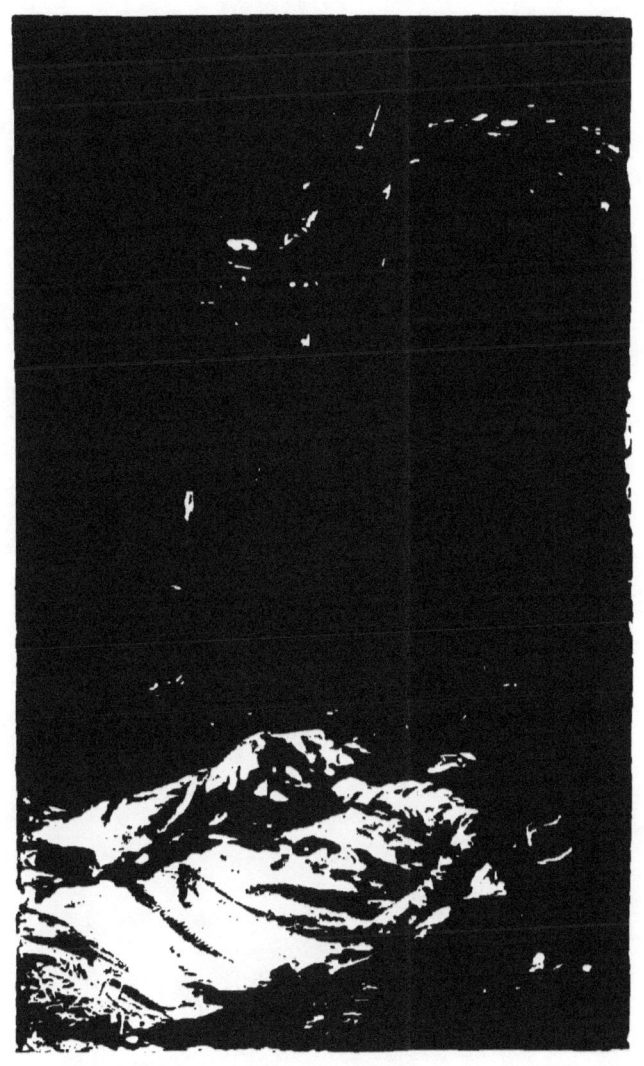

"THE WARY FEET FELT THEIR WAY DOWN THE LADDER."

ladder, and began slowly, and with the utmost caution, to descend.

The dog gave a whine and a start, tightening the cord about the arm at his side. Cliff roused instantly, put out his hand, felt the dog's head, and, patting it, told him to lie still. His eyes opened enough to see that only a few feeble flecks of moonlight rested high up on the partition, and that all was quiet in the deepening gloom of the barn; then he slept again.

During this slight disturbance, and for some minutes afterward, the figure on the ladder remained perfectly motionless against the side of the load. Then it put out a hand in the direction of the dog, and waved it with an expressive downward gesture. From that time Sparkler made neither sound nor movement. The wary feet felt their way down the ladder, and Algernon K. Winslow stood upon the barn floor.

XXXIII

"WHAT MAN-TRAP IS THAT?"

TANDING so close to the load of hay that he might have been taken for a part of it, the dog-seller contemplated the situation. The great door of the barn was before him; but to get at the fastening it would have been almost necessary for him to step over the sleeping boys, so far did their legs stretch out beyond the end of the load.

Quint's prominent features were distinctly visible in the dim, diffused light. His face was pale, and the shut eyelids, with the discolored bruise on his temple, gave it a sad and stern expression, even in sleep. He lay on his back, with one relaxed arm on his breast, the other outstretched on the blanket, and with his shoes and hat beside him on the floor.

Nearer the silent standing figure lay Cliff, turned over on the arm to which the cord was attached, with his face toward Sparkler, curled up close by on the hay. Cliff's hat and shoes were under the corner of the load, at Winslow's

216

very feet. All this the keen eye of the observer took in, even to the slender, serpent-like coil of gray cord about the dark sleeve.

He looked at the great door, then down at the legs in his way, and the eyes that would open, if they opened at all, upon any object moving in that direction. Thanks to good Mr. Payson's overheard explanations, he had knowledge of another door in the rear of the barn. He stooped to give Sparkler a quieting caress on the neck, and to look into his slyly blinking eyes, then glided away to make discoveries.

With movements so furtive that, if they had been heard, nothing more than the presence of mice on the littered floor would have been suspected, he passed the load of hay, groped his way around the carriage beyond, and found the door he sought. He had no difficulty in slipping the bolt without noise, and in opening the door a little space, to see that his way of escape was clear. It was bright starlight without; the moon was near its setting, if not already set.

Leaving the door open a good arm's-breadth, he stole back toward the front of the barn, observing every turn, and every obstacle to be avoided in any precipitate retreat. Within half a yard of Cliff's head, he got down upon his hands and knees, under the corner of the load of hay. It was darker now, and the faces of the sleepers were indistinct in shadow; but their steady breathing reassured him, and he advanced his hand until he felt the cord.

He took out his knife, with intent to cut it; but something harder than hemp stayed his blade.   Wire!—a long, flexible piece, encircling the cord, and extending from a small loop at the dog's collar to a larger one at the boy's wrist.

Upon making this discovery, he was minded to cut the collar; but the boy was sleeping so heavily that he decided to unbuckle it.   This he did without difficulty, and, having freed it from both cord and wire, he put it into his pocket.

He was now ready to depart, and to take the dog with him; but he must first devise some means of forestalling pursuit.   He crept by the cushions that pillowed the boys' heads, and reached till his groping hand touched Quint's shoes.   These he took, with the hat, and, creeping back, placed them beside Cliff's hat and shoes.   It was so dark that he had to perform his operations mostly by the sense of touch, for which circumstance he was consoled by the greater certainty it afforded him of eluding detection in the event of either of the sleepers awaking.

He was now ready for his last and most ingenious device, which he could n't think of, even at that critical moment, without a chuckle of delight.

"Since he 's so determined to hold something, I 'll oblige him," he thought, as he carried the released end of the cord toward the nearest wagon-wheel, meaning to make it fast to the rim, "so he sha'n't wake up and feel he has been wasting his time!"

But that very large substitute for the dog's collar was

too far away to permit a turn of the cord to be taken about it, without a coil or two from Cliff's arm, which could be had only at the risk of disturbing his slumber. Winslow thereupon produced from his pocket another piece, which he had not found it necessary to part with, and was about to cut off enough for his purpose when another happy thought struck him.

"No use being mean about a little string!" His position, kneeling on the barn floor, was becoming irksome, and having knotted his cord to Cliff's, he rose to his feet. Then, instead of tying it to the wagon-wheel, he drew it along, and made it fast to the ladder, quite at his leisure. "To make things lively for 'em, if they start off in a hurry!" was his amiable purpose.

So far, all was well, from his own point of view, although our boys, if they had been awake to the situation, might have regarded it differently. He was prepared to resume his career in a gullible world, only one other slight precaution remaining to be taken.

He would have stolen their clothes, if that had been possible. As it was, he could make free only with their hats and shoes.

The hats, one after the other, he tossed upon the load of hay, where they lodged noiselessly. All this time the dog had lain as still as the sleeping boys; but now, at a signal from his master, he crouched on his paws, alert and intelligent, awaiting orders. Then in one hand Winslow gathered all the shoes except one; this he gave to Sparkler to carry, and with that too faithful accomplice stole away, as silent as the shadows amid which they passed.

And still the tired Biddicut boys slept on.

At this juncture an astonishing thing occurred.

As Winslow approached the door, which he had left unlatched and slightly ajar, he was startled to see it fly all at once wide open, as if moved by an unseen hand. He stopped, half expecting a human form to appear in the square of starlit space suddenly confronting him. But all was strangely quiet, and it seemed for a moment as if the door had opened magically, of its own accord, to let him pass.

The mystery was quickly solved; a wind was rising, and it had carried the outward-swinging door around on its hinges. He foresaw what might happen next, and hastened forward to prevent it. But he was too late. A counter-gust swung the door again, shutting it with a loud, rattling bang.

An indescribable hubbub ensued. The boys started up with cries of amazement, demanding of each other what had happened.

"It was a door that slammed!" exclaimed Quint.

"Somebody has been in the barn!" cried Cliff, feeling hurriedly for the dog.

"Where in thunder are my shoes?" Quint roared.

"The dog! The dog is gone!" said Cliff, in wild consternation. "He's here, though!"

He was on his feet, following up the cord, which was

certainly attached to something, but which seemed to be miraculously lengthened, as if it had grown in the night.

"Jehu! what 's all this?"

His hand encountered the wired knot that had clasped Sparkler's collar; but instead of the collar he found more cord—more cord!

"The old Harry has been here!" he wailed, in mad bewilderment.

"It 's the old Winslow!" said Quint. In springing up he had struck his head a stunning blow against the projecting frame of the hay-wagon; but without heeding the hurt, or waiting to find his shoes, he started for the door that had made the bang, and which was now slowly swinging open again.

In his headlong rush he passed between his friend and the load of hay.

"Look out!" Cliff implored. But Quint kept on, plunging over the cord, dragging Cliff after him, and bringing the ladder down upon both their backs. If Winslow had remained to witness the unqualified success of his scheme for making things "lively" in the deacon's barn, he would have had no cause to complain of the result.

"What man-trap is that?" muttered Quint, as he scrambled off, freeing his legs from the cord and his back from the encumbrance of the ladder, and made for the open door.

It had taken the dazed Cliff some moments to assure

himself that there was no dog at the other end of the
cord; but he was thoroughly satisfied of the fact by this
time. His shoulder had received a staggering blow from
the tumbling ladder, and his wrist a tremendous wrench
from the sharply drawn, wire-wound loop; but he quickly
disengaged himself from both, and forgot his hurts in
the fury that possessed him to rush out in pursuit of the
author of his woes.

XXXIV

ANOTHER MYSTERIOUS MAN-TRAP

UTSIDE the barn he found night and silence, the dim earth outspread, and the starry universe—nothing more. Not a footstep was heard; not a human figure was seen, not even Quint's.

"Quint, where are you?" Cliff called out in a thrilled voice, standing bareheaded amid the great mystery into which he had rushed.

Then something which might have been a post detached itself from a fence near by and moved toward him. It was the shoeless Quint.

"Which way did he go?" Cliff demanded.

"That's more than I know," Quint replied. "He was out of sight and hearing before I pitched out of the door. I thought I heard a heavy, thumping sound, but I've no idea in which direction."

"I can't understand it!" said Cliff. "I'm sure somebody went out of the barn, not ter seconds before you did."

"Ten seconds is a good while when you are racing with the old Scratch!" Quint said. Both listened. "It does seem as if I should have heard him running!"

"I believe he has dropped into a hiding-place somewhere," said Cliff; "or he is half a mile away by this time. That dog! that dog!" he moaned, in angry despair. "Just after we had found out about him, and I was so sure of holding fast to him this time!"

"The ground will be wet and soft, and we can track 'em by daylight," said Quint. "I don't see what else we can do. He must have been in the barn when Mr. Payson locked us in."

"That's what the dog's strange actions meant," replied Cliff. "What a fool, that I did n't suspect it! You remember how he tried to bounce up the ladder? Winslow must have heard all our talk!"

"Did he take your shoes, too?" Quint inquired.

"I guess so; I did n't stop to hunt."

They paused frequently to listen during this whispered talk. They seemed to be in a large yard, partly surrounded by a fence, which on one side was connected with a corner of the barn by a gate. Beyond the gate was a driveway, which Winslow would probably have taken if he had made at once for the street. But the gate was closed and hooked.

"He never would have stopped to hook it," said Cliff.

"Nor to open it," argued Quint.

The gate was constructed of horizontal strips of board, with spaces between; the fence was similar, and low enough to be easily scaled by a man, or leaped by a dog of Sparkler's abilities; or the dog might even have crept between the boards.

The boys were searching for some sign to guide them, when Cliff's foot hit some dark object lying loose among the sparse weeds and stunted grass by the fence. It was so much like a shoe that he stooped and picked it up. And a shoe it was.

"Mine, I do believe!" he declared.

"Look for more," said Quint. "We may track 'em by our own shoes!"

"Here 's another, and another!" said Cliff, "all right here by the fence!"

"This is the way he went; he dropped the shoes as he jumped over."

Beyond the fence was an open space, lying between Mr. Payson's house and an apple-orchard not far off. The boys concluded that Winslow had vanished among the trees. Once in their shade, he could steal away without being seen or heard. Cliff sprang upon the fence; Quint stood looking over it.

"What 's that?" Cliff whispered, intently gazing and listening. "Coming toward us!"

"A dog?" Quint suggested.

"A dog, as sure as I am crazy!" said Cliff, in wild excitement; for what he saw appeared too marvelous to be true.

He jumped down from the fence to meet the returning truant.

"Sparkler! It's Sparkler!" he cried, darting forward to seize him.

But Sparkler had no intention of allowing himself to be so easily recaptured. As Cliff advanced he retreated, turning and capering as if to lead him on; and when Quint came up, he ran away toward some dark object lying on the ground. Just then, from that direction, came a horrible groan.

"Jehu mighty! what's that?" said Cliff, his imagination conjuring up appalling mysteries in the strange night scene they were exploring.

"We'll see what it is!" exclaimed Quint, striding eagerly forward over the wet turf.

The dark object became a man, and rose to a sitting posture. The dog leaped upon him, then ran back toward the boys, who were now within a few paces of the spot.

The ground was level, with no visible impediment anywhere; and yet here was a human being struggling up with pain and difficulty from the ground, upon which he had evidently fallen, from no discernible cause—the human being they sought!

Even Quint was startled by the strangeness of the chance that had so suddenly and mysteriously interrupted Winslow's hasty flight. What could have happened to him? Why that dreadful groan? And why had he permitted his presence to be betrayed by the very dog he was hurrying away?

The shadowy orchard was on the left; on the right were the kitchen porch and rear gable of the Payson

"THE DARK OBJECT BECAME A MAN."

house, only two or three rods distant. The boys slack-
ened their speed,—very fortunately, as it proved,—and
advanced cautiously, peeringly, along the open space,
toward the man, who was by this time struggling to get
upon his feet.

"No hurry! We 've got him, sure!" said Quint.

Seeing the boys close upon him, Winslow sank down
again, resting upon his knees.

"My young friends," he said, in a badly shaken tone
of voice, "the luck is against me!"

"What are you saying your prayers here for?" Quint
demanded.

"That 's what I 'm trying to find out," Winslow
answered, feeling his head and shoulders with both
hands in a dazed sort of way. "I was running—just
skipping along about as fast as I could go,—it seemed to
be a clear course,—when all at once—"

He paused, turning his head tentatively, as if to make
sure that the joints were still in working condition.

"What happened?" Quint inquired, bending over him.

"I 've had my throat cut and my neck broken! I was
caught by a lasso, and jerked up and over, and whirled in
the air, and dropped on my back—which is another part
of me that 's badly damaged! I feel as if I 'd had a tussle
with the Old Boy himself!"

Uttering these words disconnectedly, the dog-seller
looked up and around, and felt his neck again, as if trying to realize the kind of calamity that had befallen him.

"Shall I tell you what did it?" said Quint.

"You 'll oblige me," said Winslow, his eye following the motion of the boy's lifted hand.

"You tried to cut off your useless head with this galvanized-wire clothes-line—do you see it?—running between these two posts."

"The posts I see, and I 'll take your word for the wire clothes-line!" It seemed painful for the injured man to look upward. "I 've proof enough that it 's there!"

"It 's a wonder it did n't kill you!" Quint exclaimed.

"Where 's this dog's collar?" cried Cliff, who had succeeded in catching Sparkler.

"In my waterproof-pocket, I suppose; at least, I put it there."

It was produced, and Cliff replaced it on the dog's neck.

"Did he bring you to me?" Winslow inquired.

"Sparkler? Yes," said Cliff. "He seemed to know you were in trouble and needed help."

"I was in trouble, fast enough," said Winslow; "but I could have dispensed with the help. Now, what do you propose to do?"

"Bring a doctor, if you need one," replied Quint.

"No doctor for me!"

"Then a policeman."

"Worse yet! Of the two, I prefer the doctor every time," said Winslow. "But this is n't a case for either. Boys, can't we go back into the barn there, and talk this little business over in an amicable sort of way? You need n't try to hold him,"—to Cliff, who was attaching his handkerchief to the dog's collar. "You 've got him,

and, with the help of a slamming door and a wire clothes-
line, you 've got me. That 's the mournful fact, my young
friends. I am yours to command. All I ask is, be reasonable. Oh, yes, I can walk. Thanks! "— as Quint
handed him his hat, which he picked up from the ground.

"Perhaps you can tell us where our hats are," Quint
said; "and the other half of my pair of shoes! I found
only one."

"I 'll square the shoe account, and the hat account, and
all the other accounts, to your entire satisfaction," Winslow replied. "Only give me a chance."

"And how about the tumble you gave me in the
woods?"

"I 've had a worse tumble!—such a jar, and a wrench,
and a shaking up generally as I never had before in all
the ups and downs of my varied career," said Winslow,
on his feet, and clasping the wire that had come so nigh
cutting the said career tragically short. "I reckon you 're
about even with me, boys!"

"We mean to be," said Quint, "before we get through
with you."

XXXV

THEY were walking back toward the barn, Winslow assisted by an arm Quint had passed through one of his, Cliff leading Sparkler by his handkerchief tied to the dog's collar.

The way was clear before them, surrounding objects becoming distinct. The darkness that precedes the dawn was dissolving by such delicate degrees that the change from minute to minute was unnoticeable. The east was brightening behind the orchard-trees. Then, in the orchard's edge, as they passed, a robin piped suddenly his familiar note among the boughs overhead. Another answered near by. Then a song-sparrow trilled ecstatically, other tuneful throats joined in, and soon the whole choir of field and orchard birds burst into song.

The boys were not so absorbed in the sordid business of the moment as not to feel the beauty and freshness and melody that ushered in the daily miracle of the dawn.

232

All the doubts of the night-time passed away; their sense
of the morning was one with the hope and joy that filled
their hearts.   The object of their journey was accom-
plished, or nearly so, and soon they would be on their
triumphant homeward way.

When they reached the fence, Winslow got over into
the yard, still carefully guarded by Quint.   As Sparkler
could n't leap back while confined by the handkerchief,
Cliff handed him over to his friend, then got over himself.

"The missing shoe, the first thing," said Quint, finding
the other three where he and Cliff had left them.

"If you 'll give the dog a chance, he 'll find it," said
Winslow.   "He had the handling of that one.   You
need n't be afraid to let him go; he 'll come back while
you have me."

"I won't risk it," Cliff replied.   "He and you are up to
too many tricks."

"To convince you of my good will—here, Sparkler!"
said Winslow, directing the dog's attention to the shoe in
Quint's hand, "find!"

As the dog began to pull the handkerchief in the direction of the barn, Cliff followed him to the plank-way that
sloped up to the rear door, under the edge of which
Sparkler thrust his nose and brought out the missing
shoe.

"You would n't have found it without his help—and
mine," said Winslow, eager to gain credit with his captors.

"No; and I should n't have lost it without his help—
and yours!" Quint replied.

14

The boys did n't stop to put on their shoes, but made Winslow carry back into the barn the three which he had carried out of it, while Sparkler likewise did penance by transporting the other in his teeth.

"Now, here 's a kind of string puzzle, which you can amuse yourself by undoing," said Quint, "if you are feeling well enough."

"Oh, that!" replied the dog-seller, with a feeble attempt at jocoseness. "When I took the cord from Sparkler's collar, I wanted to put it where it would do the most good, so I pieced it out and tied it to the ladder. It seems to have got into a tangle."

"Untangle it!" commanded Quint.

Obeying with cheerful docility, Winslow began loosening knots from the fallen ladder. As soon as he had freed the end of the cord, Quint made a noose in it, which he immediately slipped over the dog-seller's wrist and drew tight.

"You are not going to do such an ungentlemanly thing as that!" Winslow remonstrated, taken unawares.

"If that 's what you call ungentlemanly, you set the example," Quint replied. "I had iron on my wrists, thanks to you; and you are going to have hemp on yours, thanks to me."

"Before going any further," said the dog-seller, "allow me to make a proposition."

"We 'll hear that by and by," said Quint. "Just now, please help my chum about those other knots."

The broadening daylight, coming in through the wide-open door, shone upon a strange group there in Deacon Payson's barn. Quint held the cord, one end of which was fast to his captive's wrist, while his captive undid the knots of his own tying which united the two cords. Then Cliff, on his knees, turned Sparkler's head toward the door, and held him, while Winslow unbuckled the collar, slipped it through the small wire-wound loop, and buckled it again, both boys looking on to see that the thing was honestly done.

"You see, young gentlemen," said the dog-seller, never once losing his assurance or betraying any sense of his humiliation, "I am doing everything I can to oblige you, trusting you will reciprocate. Now, I sha'n't even wait for you to ask me where your hats are. I 'm still pretty stiff, but if my cracked joints are equal to the effort, please give me a little freedom of the cord, and I 'll restore the missing articles."

He took the ladder from the floor, and, replacing it against the load of hay, put one hand on his back, and the other on his windpipe, and begged to be allowed to breathe a moment.

"I was deucedly shaken up by that lasso business!" he remarked, with a dreary grimace.

"You are getting over it faster than I thought you would," said Quint. "Take your time. You must have been in the barn when we came into it."

"That 's a natural and just conclusion"; and the dog-seller frankly explained how he had got in. "I overheard all your talk, and I was pleased with the ingenuity of your

plans. If it had n't been for the dog, I should have left
you, undisturbed, to waylay me in the shed. As it was,
I thought you would appreciate the means I took to let
you know who had been your room-mate. Now, a little
rope, Brutus ! "

So saying, he mounted the ladder, drawing after him
the cord still attached to his wrist, Quint paying it out
through his fingers, as he looked up, with a humorous
smile, to observe the dog-seller proceeding on his extraordinary errand. Cliff, too, stood watching the movement ; and Sparkler's soft, bright eyes were also upturned,
with an expression of intelligence almost human.

From the top of the ladder Winslow stepped upon the
load of hay, Quint mounting a round or two, at his
request, to "give him more rope." Having picked up
both hats, he descended the ladder, holding them by the
rims.

"It has cost me a pang," he remarked, "for I feel as
though every bone in my body had been run through a
stone-crusher ! But anything to oblige ! The fact is,
Brutus and Cassius, I am not the unconscionable scamp
my conduct may have led you to suppose, and I am bound
to do what I can to atone for the errors I have been betrayed into by the stress of circumstances. So allow me
the pleasure—this is yours, I believe, Brutus ! Cassius,
with my compliments ! "—handing the hats with the airy
politeness which not even the "lasso business" had
shaken out of him.

As Quint put on his hat he was reminded of the ugly

bruise he had got in the tumble the man now in his power had given him. He gathered up the cord, and laid hold of his captive's unbound wrist. Winslow remonstrated.

"Have I done nothing to earn your confidence, but you still contemplate so—excuse me for saying it—so brutal a thing as that? I was just going to make my proposition."

"We'll hear your proposition," said Quint.

"Thanks, ever so much! And will you kindly allow me to recline against this ladder?" The dog-seller practically answered his own question by settling himself on the rungs. "My accident has left me as loose-jointed as a jumping-jack."

Quint suspected some crafty pretense in this; but he was willing his captive should play the jumping-jack as long as he himself held the string.

XXXVI

SETTLING WITH THE DOG-SELLER

Y proposition is to pay you the twenty dollars I agreed to, and take back the dog," said the smiling Winslow.

"You had a fair chance to make that settlement," replied Quint. "Now it's too late. We are going to have our money, but you are not going to have the dog."

"We know whose dog it is," spoke up Cliff, sitting on a box, and drying his feet with hay before putting on his shoes.

The captive persisted in his smile, though it showed rather ghastly in the morning light, and asked politely:

"Will you have the kindness to inform me how you came by that interesting information?"

"You dropped it from your pocket when you reached for your knife to use on me," replied Quint.

"And I picked it up!" cried Cliff, showing the engraved plate that had so evidently been removed from the dog-collar.

238

"You are giving it to me pretty straight, boys," the captive admitted, grinning at the metal, while his free hand pressed his pocket.

"It 's a good deal straighter than what you gave us about the burnt hotel and your sick mother in Michigan," Cliff said, returning the polished piece of nickel to his pocket.

"The burnt hotel was, I acknowledge, a myth," the captive answered. "But the sick mother, boys," he went on, with a change of tone, "she—well—I can't talk about her! Only—I 'll tell you this: I 've as good a mother as ever a bad boy had!"

Quint, too, sat on the box, preparing to put on his shoes.

"Then how happens it—" he began.

"I know what you are about to ask," said Winslow, nursing with his free hand the cord-encircled wrist, and speaking in the deeper tone into which his feeling had surprised him. "How does any son of a good mother ever go wrong? I 'll tell you what the trouble was in my case. I wanted to have the earth without paying for it. See?"

"No; I don't see," replied Cliff, with a growing interest which he was afraid might degenerate into pity. He was determined not to be guilty of that weakness.

"I 'll explain. My mother was indulgent—too indulgent. But she was poor. It was all she could do to give me a fair education, but she did that. I think you 'll allow that I have the language and breeding of a gentle-

man"; and a smirk of pride came back into the dog-
seller's pale face.

"People's ideas of a gentleman differ," said Quint.
"You 've got the gift of the gab; I won't dispute that."

"I suppose I deserve that sarcastic cut," said the captive, with a sad expression; "but it shuts off the gift—if
I have it."

"Let him tell his story," Cliff interposed, resolved be-
forehand not to believe half of it.

"Of course," Quint assented; "though when he talks
of the breeding of a gentleman after playing us such
low-down tricks—but never mind!"

"Is your mother really sick?" Cliff inquired.

"Yes—sick with the bad-son complaint!" Winslow
exclaimed. "And she 'll have it worse than ever if she
hears what I 've been up to lately. The truth is just here,
boys. I got into gay habits; I wanted more money than
she could afford me; I would n't work for it; and the
result was, I left home under what you may call a cloud.
I *have* been a hotel clerk, and I have been a good many
other things, but nothing very long at a time. I 've been
an actor—light comedy; and I 've been in the show business—employed in Barnum's Circus, boys!" he added
boastfully.

"I 'll believe *that*," said Cliff.

"That was my last situation, and I ought to have kept
it," the captive continued. "But I was foolish; I got the
idea that I was a bigger man than P. T. Barnum himself.
Unfortunately, Barnum did n't see it in that light, and

when I tried to run my end of the show in a way that did n't suit P. T., there was a little rumpus, and I found myself on the wrong side of the canvas. The trick-dog was one of my specialties, and it did n't require much of a trick to take him with me."

He looked down at Sparkler, who was looking up wistfully at him, wagging his sympathetic tail.

"Whatever you may think of *me*, boys, *he* is genuine all through—the best friend I ever had!" Winslow actually sniffed a little as he said this. "I had no thought of selling him when I started out; but necessity was the mother of that scheme. I had to raise money, and that was the way I raised it. I found it worked well, and I worked it for all it was worth. I could have made it more profitable but for one thing. Men who had money and brains too, and knew what such a dog was really worth, were—in short—suspicious. Then, I could n't sell him in the big towns without too much danger of losing him; so I played him off on the rustic population."

"My father knew he was stolen!" Cliff exclaimed.

"That 's a mistake," the captive remonstrated. "I had the care of the dog, and when I left, he left too. I kept clear of the law in that."

"But not in selling him over and over again!" Quint averred sternly, seizing his unbound wrist.

"Now, see here!" said the captive. "If you march me to the police-station, and enter a complaint, what do you gain?"

We 're going to stop your little business of swindling ' the rustic population,' " Quint declared. " We 'll gain so much ! "

"Don't be too hard on me, boys," Winslow entreated; " I 've made a clean breast of it "; and he really seemed to think his confidences entitled him to their favorable consideration. "Put yourselves in my place. *You* 've got good mothers, and one of *you* may be in a bad fix sometime."

"He 's trying the sentimental game," Quint said, with a frowning look at Cliff. "Are we going to be humbugged by him, with our eyes open ? "

"No ! " Cliff replied. "But I don't see the good of giving him over to the police. He can't sell the dog any more; and he 'll give us our money."

"Here it is, waiting for you ! " Winslow exclaimed, producing his pocket-book with alacrity. " Here 's your twenty dollars ! "—putting a roll of bills into Cliff's hand. "And I swear to return the dog to Barnum's Circus ! "

"We ought to have as much as this, after all our trouble," said Cliff, looking at the money; "but *you* are not going to return him to Barnum's Circus; I 'm not going to give up Sparkler to you for one minute; am I, Quint ? "

"That 's judgmatical," said Quint, with stern satisfaction. "If we want Barnum to have his property again, we should be fools to trust *him* to restore it."

WINSLOW'S POCKET-KNIFE

INSLOW begged them to "stick to the bargain" and give him the dog; then, finding they would not do this, he insisted upon Cliff's handing back to him ten dollars of the money.

"What do you think, Quint?" said Cliff. "*We* are not robbers, though he tried to make *you* out one last evening. *Our* ten dollars we are bound to have, anyway; but we don't want any of the money he has robbed other people of."

"No!" exclaimed Quint; "but those other people want it, and we 'll see that they have it, as far as the extra ten dollars will go. We 'll begin with the old shoemaker and his wife; won't they be tickled! No, Cliff; don't give him back a dollar of it!"

"You are right, as you are every time!" said Cliff.

As Winslow strongly objected to this manner of settlement, Quint said:

"What right have you to complain? You are getting

off what you may call *dog-cheap!* I 'm thinking we ought to hand you over to the police, after all, for the sake of those other people; and it 's only the idea of our paying some of them that satisfies my conscience in letting you off."

Winslow reflected a moment, then stooped from his seat on the ladder, and patted Sparkler affectionately.

"We part for good, I suppose, this time! Boys," he said pathetically, "are you aware that I 'm not much more than a boy myself? I 'm not twenty-two yet, and sha'n't be till next September."

"You look older than that," said Cliff.

"So will you, at twenty-two, if you live the kind of life I 've lived. 'T is n't the right kind of life, boys, and I 'm going to quit it. Live fast, and pay to-morrow—the kind of to-morrow that never comes; that 's been my style. That 's what has brought me to this humiliation!"

The captive did n't seem to take the humiliation very much to heart, however, for he added cheerfully:

"We part friends, I trust? And now, I suppose, I can dispense with this?"—and he recommenced loosening the cord at his wrist.

"Not yet!" cried Quint. "I want to see the knife you tried to draw on me last night. Your knife!" he thundered, as Winslow answered evasively. "We have had enough of delay and palaver!"

The captive brought out reluctantly what seemed to be an ordinary but rather long pocket-knife with a single blade. As it did not open in the ordinary way, Quint examined the handle, and found in it a suspicious-looking rivet, which he pressed, with a surprising result. A slender, dirk-shaped blade flew out like a flash in the morning light, and he held a deadly weapon in his hand.

"Jehu! that 's dangerous!" Cliff ejaculated, with a horrified backward start. "Think what he would have done to you last night!"

"If I had known what you really meant to do with me, you never would have got me into this shape!" muttered the prisoner.

"Think so?" said Quint, good-humoredly. "One of us was enough for you last night, and you have had us both to deal with this morning. Besides, you had been mon-keying with a galvanized-wire clothes-line."

"For my part, I feel as if we had been almost too easy with him," said Cliff, "though we might be easier still, if it was n't for the knife. I never can forgive that!"

"But we are doing this chiefly in self-defense," said Quint, giving a final tug at his hard knots. He gave a cruel laugh as he turned upon the owner of the knife. "That 's the sort of ladybird you are!" he said, with grim irony.

"I declare to you, I never used it, and never meant to!" said Winslow.

"And I declare you never shall!"

So saying, Quint drove the blade into the partition behind him, and snapped it short off. The stub that was left he pressed into a crack, where it stuck.

"None of that!"—as the captive was again at work

loosening the cord. At the same time Quint seized his other wrist.

"It serves him right!" said Cliff, shuddering at the thought of what his friend had escaped the night before.

Quint drew the bound wrist behind the ladder, and drew its fellow around the other way to meet it.

"No nonsense!" he cried, as his captive resisted. "If you prefer the police-station, all right! But do you think I 'm going to leave you to follow on our track, and keep the dog in sight till you can contrive some plot for getting him back again? By thunder!" he roared out, "if you don't stop working your wrists, we 'll march you to the station instanter! You tied my partner to the ladder; now it 's your turn."

"I hoped," said the prisoner, yielding because he must —"I hoped I had gained your confidence, and I expected more honorable treatment."

"It will take something besides your cheap talk to gain much confidence with us; and it 's droll to hear *you* preach about honorable treatment! How 's this, Cliff?"

Quint showed the prisoner's hands bound behind him and lashed to the ladder in knots above the utmost reach of his fingers, wriggle how they might. Then, taking a turn with the remainder of the cord about the captive's waist and back again, he made another knot in it, and tied the end to the ladder in a cluster of knots, which Cliff regarded with satisfaction.

"I 've heard of jugglers getting out of such tangles," he said; "but they did n't have J. Q. A. Whistler to tie the knots! If he follows us very soon, it will be with the ladder on his back."

The captive continued to protest and entreat; but Quint only said:

"My partner was very near being taken in by your humble confessions and fine promises; but they won't hurt anybody now, and they won't do you any good. Talk away, if it will amuse you. Try to console yourself for our absence. I know it will be a sad thing for you to see the last of my gambrel-roof nose!"

He was fastening the rear door. This done, the two Biddicut boys, accompanied by Sparkler, went out by the great front door, which they closed after them, leaving Winslow lashed to the ladder in the lonesome barn.

XXXVIII

HOMEWARD BOUND

S they were passing near Deacon Pay-
son's kitchen porch, they were delighted
to see the deacon himself coming out of
the door.

"Starting so early?" said the good
man. "I'd been hearing voices, and I
thought I'd come out and see how you had got through
the night."

Then, if ever there was an amazed old gentleman at
four o'clock on a fine summer morning, it was the worthy
deacon, standing beside his kitchen porch and listening
to the story of the strange happenings in his barn and
orchard.

"My wife said she heard the voices outdoors first, but
she did n't wake me. That wire clothes-line must have
been a savage thing to run afoul of! No wonder it
floored him! And he 's in the barn there now? I never
heard anything so surprising!"

"We think he 'd better stay there an hour or so," said
Cliff; "then do what you please with the fellow."

"We make you a present of him," said Quint, "only hoping he won't give you much trouble."

"I 'll leave him till my man comes; then, I suppose, we 'd better cut him loose—though I 'm inclined to think," said the deacon, "that he ought to be put in pickle for all his misdemeanors. Come into the house," he went on; "you can't start off this way, on empty stomachs."

He made the boys go in, which they did very willingly, and talked over with them their homeward trip, while his wife set before them butter and bread and cold sliced veal, and glasses of milk, and amber honey dripping from the comb, Sparkler also receiving a share. Then they took leave of these kind people, listened for sounds in the barn as they went out, but heard none, and set off in the cool morning air, on the clean-washed country roads, with the light of the new-risen sun on their glad faces.

Winslow did not follow them, with or without the ladder on his back, and they never saw him again.

The boys were minded to make directly for the nearest way-station on the railroad connecting with the Biddicut branch. But it was early for trains, and remembering their promise to Mr. Mills, they determined to take his house on their way, and report to him the success of their expedition. Perhaps they also wished to enjoy their triumph in the merry eyes of the two girls who had been so mischievously inclined to laugh at them.

They found a shorter course than the one by which they had hunted Winslow, and reached the farm-house just as the family were sitting down at table. They were

15

heartily welcomed, and offered a second breakfast, which they accepted with frank good will, and paid well for the hospitality in the entertainment the tale of their adventures afforded. There was open admiration as well as merriment in the bright eyes of the girls opposite them, as the boys took turns in the narrative, Cliff rendering the more dramatic portions in his impulsive way, and Quint setting off the whole with his droll commentary.

The meal over, Cliff would have had Sparkler perform some of his tricks. But the dog had also had a second breakfast, or his last parting with his late master had sobered him too much, or he resented the restraint of the cord, of which Cliff would on no account relieve him. Whatever the cause, he was in one of his dumpish moods, and would do nothing.

Then Cliff took from his pocket five dollars of the money recovered from Winslow, and handed them to Mr. Mills for the old shoemaker, whom the farmer promised to see and reimburse for his loss within a few days.

"Now, I have five dollars which I must manage to get to Mr. Miller of Wormwood," said Cliff. "Plenty more dog-purchasers may turn up, and there won't be money enough to go around; so, first come, first served."

Having kept the boys as long as he could, the farmer offered to harness a horse and drive them over to a station on the connecting road, which favor they gratefully accepted, and the wagon was brought to the door. Cliff lifted Sparkler into it, the dog refusing to jump, made

"CLIFF WOULD HAVE HAD SPARKLER PERFORM"

him lie down on the bottom, and got in after him, along with Quint.

Then adieus were said, and smiles exchanged; the girls waved their handkerchiefs, and the boys their hats; the farmer touched up his nag, and our Biddicut adventurers felt that they were indeed on their way home.

They drove briskly along the green-bordered country roads, where every wayside bush and tree glistened in the early sunshine.

"No stop now till we see Biddicut!" Cliff said exultantly, "only as we may have to wait for trains."

"I would n't stop now," observed Quint, "even to make a friendly call on Winslow working his passage in Deacon Payson's barn."

Yet it was n't long before both boys called out simultaneously for a halt, as they were passing another barn, on their way through a small town.

It was a weather-worn structure, all of a dreary brown hue, except as to one end, which was conspicuously and garishly red with enormous posters advertising the incomparable attractions of Barnum's combined circus and menagerie—the "Greatest Show on Earth." There were pictures of monkeys at their tricks, a half-naked man grappling with a lion, a tiger pouncing upon a sleeping Arab, elephants playing at see-saw or balancing themselves on rolling balls, and athletes in all sorts of startling and impossible positions, linked together, or leaping, or falling head foremost through the air.

"They ought to have Sparkler here somewhere," said

Cliff.   But the boys searched in vain among the flaming
marvels for a performing dog; and when Cliff pulled
Sparkler up from the bottom of the wagon, and tried to
interest him in the supposed representations of his companions of the show, he regarded them with the utmost
indifference, and dropped down again, blinking sleepily,
upon his paws.

"Here's what we want to know!" exclaimed Quint, out
of the wagon, confronting the red-gabled barn, and studying the dates and names of places advertising the succes-
sive appearances of the "Greatest Show on Earth."

XXXIX

BACK IN BIDDICUT

"E'S coming! Cliff is coming! And he's got the dog! He's bringing home the dog!"

Trafton Chantry, who had been watching at the gate for his absent brother, shrieked out this announcement at about nine o'clock that morning, and immediately started for the house, as if running a race with his own voice.

The voice got there first, and Susie took up the cry: "Cliff is coming! Cliff is coming with the dog!" She flew through the kitchen and out of it, calling, "Amos, he's come! Tell pa, quick! He's come with the dog!"

The mother, who was doing some work in the pantry, dropped whatever was in her hands, and hastened to the door to behold with her own amazed and happy eyes the return of the wanderer, of whom no word had been received since Quint's father brought news of the two boys the day before. Very great had been her concern for him during all the dragging hours of the night and morning, and her joy at sight of him returning, proud and successful, after all her fears, was too much for dry eyes.

"I declare," she exclaimed, "wonders will never cease! My son! and he has got the prize!" For to her also the appearance of the dog led captive was the crowning triumph of her boy's return.

Trafton had rushed out again to meet his brother, and they came into the yard together, walking fast, and talking fast, with Sparkler trotting demurely between them. Amos came running and shouting, and Mr. Chantry appeared, his amused face quirking between his fleecy side-whiskers; and soon a jubilant group was gathered, of which Cliff was the central figure and flushed hero.

He stood holding Sparkler by the cord, and with gleeful excitement answering, or attempting to answer, the volleys of questions of which he was the target.

"Pa said he'd bet a thousand dollars you would n't bring home any dog," cried Amos, glorying in his brother's glory.

"I wish I could have taken that bet!" Cliff retorted, while the father stood parting his whiskers with both hands, and smiling with good-humored sarcasm.

"I did n't think you would get him," he said; "and I did n't see much use in it, even if you should. 'T would take a good many dogs to pay for the anxiety your mother suffered, sitting up for you last night, or lying awake for you."

"I thought of that," Cliff replied; "and I would have helped it, if I could."

HOME AT LAST!

"That's nothing now," said his mother. "Your father was just as anxious as I was. But we both had faith in you and Quint, that you would be able to take care of yourselves, and get home all right sometime."

"And we all said," struck in Susie, "as you did n't get home yesterday, it must have been because you had got on the track of the dog. Pa said so, too."

"Do sit down, Cliff," said his mother. "You must be tired. And we 'll all try to keep still and let you tell your story."

"I 'm not a bit tired," Cliff protested, sitting down, nevertheless; "and I don't know what to tell first. Only this I 'll say, first, and last, and all the time: I owe everything to Quint. He 's great! You never saw such a fellow! And now—" He could n't help telling the most surprising part of his story at the beginning. "If you want to know who is the real owner of the dog—see here!"

He held something clasped in his hand, which he opened under his father's peering gray eyes, watching the effect of so astonishing a revelation.

Mr. Chantry took the name-plate, regarded it curiously, and remarked coolly: "I told you the fellow stole the dog! But are you sure—"

"See how it fits the place in the collar!" cried Cliff. "And the fellow himself owned up that he stole him from the circus. He 's Barnum's famous performing spaniel!"

Any disappointment Cliff may have felt in consequence of his father's seeming lack of enthusiasm was amply compensated by the exclamations of wonder with which the others regarded the engraved plate and heard his account of how he came by it.

"P. T. Barnum" was a famous name in those days, known in every household in the land. None of the Chantry family had seen his show, which never deigned to visit small places like Biddicut; but they had heard and read much of it, and the boys had been filled with burning envy of their few more fortunate mates who had enjoyed that distinguished privilege. So that, in the minds of all, it added immensely to the importance of the dog lolling at their feet, and to the fact of Cliff's possession of him, to know that he belonged to the great traveling circus and menagerie.

XL

WHAT SHOULD BE DONE WITH HIM?

OR was Mr. Chantry's enthusiasm as unmoved as it appeared. There was a glistening brightness in his eyes as he held the plate in his hand, and glanced at it occasionally, while Cliff told his story; and finally, when he heard how the boys had followed Winslow, through hardships and discouragements, and captured him at last, he no longer attempted to disguise his satisfaction.

"I always knew Quint Whistler had good stuff in him," he remarked; "and I don't see that the other Biddicut boy's conduct was anything to be very much ashamed of. Yes, Cliff; I think you did right to take the twenty dollars, and that you and Quint had well earned all you got. But I'm glad you propose to keep only the ten you had been tricked out of. I've heard of your Mr. Miller, in Wormwood, and I'm pretty sure Quint's father knows him. We'll get his five dollars to him in some way. And now—" Mr. Chantry glanced at the engraved name again—"now about the real owner of this dog with too many owners!"

The younger boys were on their knees, patting and hugging the unconscious object of so much solicitude and excited discussion.

"Oh, we never can let him go again, if he *is* Barnum's trick-dog!" said Amos. "I would n't!"

"Can't we buy him of Barnum?" was Trafton's pathetic appeal.

"That is n't likely," said the father. "Such a dog as that is worth too much money. Barnum must be notified, the first thing. I should think a reward would be offered for him, if he really belongs to the show."

"How much do you think?" Susie inquired.

"I 've no idea," Mr. Chantry replied, parting his whiskers contemplatively. "Maybe as much as fifteen or twenty dollars."

"I would n't give him up for any such sum as that!" said Susie.

"Nor I!" "Nor I!" chimed in the younger boys, while Cliff looked thoughtfully down at the pet crouched lazily between his feet.

"It is n't a question of what you would or you would n't do," said the father; "it 's a question of what is right. Stolen property belongs to the owner, no matter what innocent hands it has fallen into. Barnum has the name of being a liberal sort of man, and whether he offers a reward or not, I 've no doubt he 'll see that you and Quint are paid for your trouble, if he cares to have the dog back again. You said you looked up the names of the places where his show is to be the next few days."

"It's in Lowell to-day," Cliff replied. "Next Monday it is to be in Worcester, and the day after in Springfield. I tell you, it was a temptation for Quint and me to go as straight to Lowell as we could, and have the business settled before there was a chance for any more accidents. But we were not sure Barnum was with the show, and we both felt the need of a change of clothes—unless, as Quint said, we wanted Barnum to engage us as something new in the way of curiosities. So we concluded it would be as well to come home, and tell the news, and consult our folks."

"A wise conclusion," said Mr. Chantry, who commonly put so much pepper in his praises of his children that any commendation of his that was free from such ironic condiment gave them all the greater satisfaction. "I don't see but you have acted, all through, about as discreetly as two boys could. Now we'll consult Quint's folks, and decide what's best to do."

"That's my idea," said Cliff; "for of course he has just as much interest in the dog now as I have. He stopped to see his folks, but he promised to come by and by, and talk the matter over."

"To-day is Saturday," Mr. Chantry mused aloud. "I believe Mr. Barnum generally travels with his show, but he may be going home to Bridgeport to spend Sunday. I don't believe a letter addressed to Lowell would find him there."

"You might telegraph," Mrs. Chantry proposed.

But Mr. Chantry had never sent or received a telegraphic

message in his life, and what to most business men would have seemed a simple and ordinary thing to do appeared to his inexperience an expensive novelty.

"I'll write to Bridgeport," said he. "If he is n't there, the letter will be forwarded. I don't know about telegraphing. A little delay may be unavoidable, but it won't do any harm."

"It seems to me," said Mrs. Chantry, "it would be a good idea for Cliff himself to write the letter; why not?"

"That's so; to be sure!" said her husband.

"Oh, I can't write a letter to Mr. Barnum!" Cliff exclaimed, looking up with frightened eyes.

"Do the best you can," said his father. "Make it as brief and businesslike as possible, without trying to tell anything more than is necessary. You never wrote a letter to a great man, and very likely you never will have another chance."

And Mr. Chantry went out, laughing, and stroking his whiskers, leaving the boy to face the formidable difficulty of the letter.

XLI

CLIFF WRITES A LETTER AND RECEIVES A TELEGRAM

OWEVER, his father's hint had set the boy's mind to working; and while putting Sparkler into the shed, and afterward when he was refreshing himself with soap and water and clean clothing, he thought out the substance of what he would write in his letter to the "great man."

"If I just say in plain words that I 've got the dog, and would like to know what to do with him, won't that be enough?" he asked his mother, as he seated himself at the sitting-room secretary and let down the desk.

"Why, that 's just what you want to say," replied his mother. "Write just as you would talk. Now, boys, don't bother him; don't ask him any more questions, but keep away till he has got his letter written."

Cliff, nevertheless, chewed his pen-handle a good deal, and started two or three letters, before he found just the "plain words" he wanted, and put them together in this way:

DEAR SIR: Two days ago a man calling himself Algernon K. Winslow came to this town, and sold me a dog for ten dollars. The dog is a small spaniel of mixed breed, and he has been trained to perform tricks. The dog got away the next morning, and another boy and I followed him through five towns, and caught him last night, and brought him home to our house this forenoon. We found the dog had been sold to several different persons, and he had got away from everybody. There was no name on the dog's collar, but we think we have proof that he belongs to you. I like the dog, and would be glad to keep him; but if he is yours, and you want him again, please let me know what you wish to have done with him.

This letter he signed in formal fashion, and showed to his mother.

"Why, Clifford," she said, "I think it is a very creditable letter, and I 'm sure your father will say so, too."

"I had no idea of writing so much, but it all came in," said Cliff, well pleased with his composition, now that his mother had commended it. "But I want to correct it and copy it before father has a chance to make fun of it. I 've got too many 'dogs' in it, for one thing; I want to take out five or six."

"I think, myself, you could improve it by striking out the word 'dog' in some places," his mother admitted. "Let 's see how it can be done."

"I 'll do it all myself," said Cliff, "so I sha'n't have to acknowledge I had help about writing just a little letter to Mr. Barnum!"

He had the letter corrected and neatly copied (for Cliff wrote a very good hand), with the word "dog" occurring in it only twice, by the time his father came in.

"Did you do all that without help from anybody?" said Mr. Chantry—the very question Cliff knew he would ask.

"Of course," said Cliff, carelessly. "I found there was n't much to say. If it is n't all right, I can try again." (The evidence of his previous trials had disappeared in the kitchen fire.)

His father gave a nod of decided approval.

"Well, Clifford, I don't mind telling you I could n't have done better myself."

"Is n't there too much of it?" said Cliff, trying to conceal his gratification.

"I don't see that there is. You tell how you came by the dog, and it 's right to say something of the trouble you had in hunting him, and to let Mr. Barnum know you would like to keep him. No!" said Mr. Chantry, emphatically; "I don't find anything in it to alter; and now we 'll see to posting it in time for the noon mail."

"I think I 'd better put on the envelop, 'Return in five days to Clifford Chantry, Biddicut, Mass.,' so that if it does n't get to Mr. Barnum it will come back to me."

"That 's businesslike—quite businesslike!" said Mr. Chantry, in full assent.

"Only I think I 'd better not seal it till Quint sees it," pursued Cliff, "since it 's his affair as much as mine."

"You are right, my boy! right in every particular!" said his father, quite forgetting that jeering habit of his, by which, without ever seriously intending it, he had embittered for his children so many occasions when a kindly word would have made them happy.

Quint came in soon after, and, being shown the letter, remarked :

"That's judgmatical! I don't see how it could be better—unless I had written it myself!"

The two boys went together to mail it in the village, which done, Cliff drew a long breath, exclaiming :

"Now, to wait for an answer! We are pretty sure none will come to-day or to-morrow, but after that Sparkler may be sent for at any time. It makes me feel blue to think of it."

"You ought to show off his tricks once more," Quint suggested. "I'd like to have my folks see him. And why not ask in a few friends?"

"I'll do it! I'll do it this very evening!" Cliff exclaimed. "Come over early, and bring along as many as you like. I'll try to have him in good condition, only a little hungry, so he sha'n't go back on us."

The entertainment took place in the Chantry sitting-room, with doors closed, and only screened windows open, and it proved delightfully successful. Quint's father and mother and sister were present, and there were, besides, a few boys of the neighborhood (Dick Swan and Ike Ingalls among them), who regarded the invitations as precious favors.

Sparkler performed his tricks, some of them over and over again, with a charming alertness that won all hearts, and made the children more than ever unwilling to part with him. During the rests between, and afterward, Cliff and Quint, in response to many questions, gave a most diverting account of their adventures, with many details which Cliff had omitted from his previous narration.

To Mr. Chantry, who sat quietly rocking and stroking his whiskers, what was most gratifying in this part of the entertainment was the generous forwardness each boy showed in attributing the chief credit of their exploit to his companion.   For of what value, after all, are victories won and prizes gained, unless the character be at the same time enriched?

Sunday was a day of delicious rest to both our Biddicut boys, and Monday, fortunately, found them ready to renew their adventure.

No letter came from Mr. Barnum; but early in the forenoon a messenger-boy from the village brought a yellowish-brown envelop, which he displayed as, with pretended ignorance, he inquired for Clifford Chantry.

"What is it?" cried Cliff, running to receive it.

"It 's a telegram," replied the boy, holding it behind him.   "Who is Mr. Clifford Chantry, anyway, and where can I find the gentleman?"

"No fooling, Bob Eldon!" said Cliff, pouncing upon the messenger, capturing the envelop, and tearing it open.

It contained a telegraphic blank, dated at Bridgeport, and filled out thus:

Deliver dog to Barnum's Circus, at Worcester to-day, or at Springfield to-morrow. Reward and expenses will be paid. P. T. BARNUM.

Cliff was reading this message, in a highly excited state of mind, when Quint arrived, having immediately followed

16

the messenger-boy, who, as he passed the Whistler premises, had yelled out the startling news that he carried a despatch for Cliff.

All the Chantry household quickly gathered to hear and discuss the momentous intelligence, and Mr. Chantry observed:

"The dog should go to-day, for you 'll have so much farther to take him to-morrow. Now, which of you boys will go? or shall I go in your place?" he asked quizzically.

"We 'll both go!" said Cliff and Quint, speaking together.

"That 's just the answer I expected," Mr. Chantry replied, laughing humorously. "And it 's my opinion, the sooner you start, the better, for I don't know about the railroad connections."

Quint hastened home to put on suitable clothes, and to be rejoined by Cliff on his way with Sparkler to the station. Cliff also prepared himself for a possible interview with the great showman, and led Sparkler out from the shed by the cord, from which he had ventured to remove the wire. All the family followed him to the gate, the parents to give him good advice, and the children to pat and hug for the last time the wonderful quadruped.

"Let me go and see him off; can't I?" pleaded Trafton.

"Me too!" cried Amos.

The granting of the request made Susie wish she was a boy, that she might claim the same privilege.

The three Chantry boys were joined by Quint as they passed the Whistler house; and as they went on, other village boys ran out to swell the procession, the surprising report having spread that Cliff had received a despatch from the great showman, and that he and Quint were on their way to return the dog to the circus at Worcester—an event that made envious youngsters wish Winslow would come along with more trick-dogs, of which they might become the purchasers.

The two partners, with their captive, did not have long to wait for the train, which relieved them of their too noisy and officious host of friends, and soon set them down at the Junction. There they had to wait for another train; and they had still one more change of cars to make, and then a ride which seemed interminable to their impatience, before they alighted at the station in Worcester.

XLII

HOW THE BOYS WENT TO THE CIRCUS

ANY people were getting out of the cars, evidently bound for the same destination with the two boys from Biddicut. Some climbed into omnibuses and wagons in waiting; others set off rapidly on foot.

"Shall we walk?" said Cliff. "We 've only to follow the crowd."

"Since our expenses are to be paid, I rather think we can afford to ride," replied Quint, as they approached a wagon bearing a placard inscribed:

"To Circus Grounds—10 cents."

They had already discussed the question whether the word in the despatch meant that expenses would be paid for as many as might come with the dog, and had decided that it could n't be strictly so construed. But they felt that their business was important, and that a little lav-

ishness of expenditure would therefore be justifiable.
Cliff took Sparkler in his arms, and, climbing to a seat in
the wagon, made him lie down between his knees; Quint
took the only other vacant place; and they were soon
passing the throngs of pedestrians, in their rapid course
to the circus grounds.

Cliff's bosom swelled mightily at sight of the great
white tents, the swaying flags, and the converging crowds,
with the blue dome of a perfect summer sky arching over
all. He turned to see if Quint's face betrayed any unusual
emotion, and Quint answered his look with a beaming smile.

They were out of the wagon almost as soon as it
stopped, and found themselves in a stream of people
before a row of small tents, or booths, containing side-
shows, the wonders of which were noisily advertised by
hand-organs, drums, and shouting men.

Avoiding the stand of the ticket-sellers, the boys made
directly for the main entrance of the circus tents. Two
men were taking tickets of the throng passing between
them. They hardly noticed anybody, and observed
neither our Biddicut boys nor the dog until, as one held
out his hand for Cliff's ticket, he received this extraordinary greeting:

"We 've come to see Mr. Barnum, if he is here."

"He is here, or will be," replied the man. "You 'll see
him when he makes his speech. Your ticket!"

"We have n't any. I—"

"Don't come here without tickets! Stand aside and
let people pass!"

Cliff held his ground, with Quint close behind him.

"I have this telegram from Mr. Barnum," he cried out, to the surprise of the entering spectators, and of the ticket-taker himself especially; "and we have brought the dog."

The man regarded Cliff more carefully, and cast his eye down at the little animal shrinking from the legs of the entering crowd.

"It's King Francis!" he said to his fellow ticket-taker. "I never expected to see him again!"

He would have taken the telegram as if it had been a ticket; but Cliff kept tight hold of it, merely allowing him to glance it over.

"You should have gone to the private entrance; but all right! Dick!" the man called to somebody within the tent, "here's King Francis back again! Go with that man!" he said to Cliff, and went on with his ticket-taking, which had hardly been interrupted.

Cliff passed into the tent, but Quint was stopped in attempting to follow him.

"He's my partner!" Cliff called back, standing aside to let the crowd pass.

"He can't go in without a ticket," the man declared. "One of you is enough to go with the dog. Pass along! pass along!"

At the same time the attendant named Dick offered to take the cord from Cliff's hand; but Cliff exclaimed:

"The dog doesn't go without me, and I don't go without my partner! We are here on Mr. Barnum's business, and if we can't—"

"Go in! go in!" said the ticket-taker, nodding at Quint; and Quint, laughing at the effect of Cliff's defiant words, quickly rejoined him in the tent.

It was a sort of vestibule to the great wild-beast show and the greater amphitheater beyond. In it were a number of living curiosities, among which the boys noticed a very tame giant stalking about, and a human mite, placed, in effective contrast with him, on a low platform, from which he shouted up at every spectator who paused, "How's the weather up where you are?"—his invariable salutation,—in a squeaking mite of a voice.

They passed on through a large circular tent redolent of wild beasts, with great iron-barred cages on either side, and a group of elephants, chained each by one foot, in the central space. There was the monarch of elephants, the mighty Jumbo, rocking himself on his hips, and dusting himself with wisps of hay which his huge, elastic, swinging trunk swept over his shoulders and back. Beyond were other trunks, like writhing and twisting anacondas, with open, upturned mouths, which they passed around like contribution-boxes, begging peanuts and bonbons of the spectators. In the cages were mischievous monkeys, restless hyenas walking to and fro, sleepy-looking lions, and beautiful pards and panthers, only glimpses of which could be had through the human groups pressing against the ropes, but which the boys promised themselves they would see more of before they left the show.

The attendant Dick looked down occasionally at the

dog Cliff persisted in leading, and made a single remark as they passed the last of the cages:

"The old man will smile to see his pet back again!"—the "old man" being, as the boys understood, the great showman himself.

The next tent was vastly larger still. It was the "mammoth tent" of the circus performances, supported by tall masts, festooned with flags, and hung, high overhead, with all the apparatus used by acrobats in their daring aërial feats. The benches, rising one above another from the ample ring, were rapidly filling with spectators; attendants were arranging spring-boards and laying mats for the tumblers; and the members of a band, wearing showy uniforms, and bearing shining instruments, some of prodigious size, were filing to their places. To the boys, who had never seen a great circus, there was in all this preparation an inspiring suggestiveness which filled them with wonder and joy.

Dick lifted the flap of a curtain, and ushered them into a side-tent, where a troop of athletes in costume and two or three fantastic clowns were gossiping together or walking about, as if waiting for their work to begin, one stepping aside, now and then, to turn a handspring or a backward somerset on the grass, in mere exuberance of spirits, hardly ceasing from his talk and laughter while whirling in the air.

Past this picturesque and interesting group Dick led the boys toward a part of the tent where a full-proportioned man in a black hat and a swallow-tailed coat, standing with his back toward them, was talking with two other men, one of whom had a ring-master's whip in his hand. The large man was speaking earnestly, and did not look around until the ring-master, seeing the boys approaching with the dog and their guide, broke out jovially:

"Ho, ho, ho! There's his Majesty! Mr. Barnum, King Francis has arrived!"

Thereupon the man in the swallow-tailed coat turned a full, genial face smilingly toward the boys, and snapped his thumb and finger at the dog. Sparkler had so far shown but little interest in anything he saw; but at this signal he dashed forward the length of his leash, leaping up, and manifesting the most joyous emotion under his real owner's caresses.

XLIII

AN INTERVIEW WITH THE GREAT SHOWMAN

"OU have got along earlier than I expected," Mr. Barnum then said, looking pleasantly at Cliff. "You've had some trouble with this good-for-nothing!—if you are the young man who wrote me the letter."

Cliff stood with his hat off, flushed and panting; but the showman's pleasant manners quickly relieved him of the embarrassment he felt on finding himself in his presence.

"I started as soon as I got your message," he replied. "This is my partner, Quincy Whistler. I never could have got the dog back if it had n't been for him; so I thought we 'd better both come and fetch him."

Quint also stood with his hat off, gravely smiling—a youth without blemish, except for the bruised spot on his left temple. Cliff noticed that the showman's comprehensive glance rested for a moment on that discoloration, and hastened to explain:

"He got that in a tussle with Winslow—the man who sold me the dog. He might have got worse, for Winslow tried to draw a knife on him."

"Winslow?" queried the showman.

"That 's one of the names he goes by," said Cliff, "though I don't suppose it is his real name. I 've brought the bill of sale he signed when he sold me the dog"—putting on his hat, and producing the paper from his pocket.

The showman glanced his eye over it with a smile that struggled with a frown.

"I know the handwriting," he said, "and I know the man. A scapegrace, if ever there was one! You are quite right; his name is not Winslow."

"He told us—not when he sold me the dog, but after we had followed him up and caught him—he told us," said Cliff, "that he had been connected with your show."

"He told the truth, for once," replied the showman. "I know his family—respectable Bridgeport people. For their sakes, I set the fellow on his feet when he was down, and gave him employment. He is smart enough; he could make himself useful, if he chose; and I engaged him at a fair salary. But it was n't safe to trust him with money, so I made him sign an agreement that all but a small part of his earnings should be reserved for the payment of his debts—chiefly debts to his own father, who has ruined himself by helping him out of scrapes. Yes,"—in answer to a question from Cliff,—"he has a good mother, a refined, intelligent woman. From his boyhood he has given them no end of trouble."

"He told us he was hardly more than a boy even now —not yet twenty-two," said Cliff.

"He is twenty-four years old," said the showman. "I'd like to retain this"—folding the bill of sale, and putting it into his pocket. "He might have kept his place in my show, but he became dissatisfied with the arrangement, and finally demanded his wages, cash in hand. Knowing he would squander every dollar I gave him, I refused—for his own good, and his family's, as he knew very well. He was intolerably conceited; he imagined the 'Greatest Show on Earth' could n't be run without his assistance. I promptly dispelled that illusion. He became impertinent, and disappeared with the dog."

"He gave us that part of the story pretty straight," observed Quint.

The showman regarded him with friendly interest, remarking:

"He's a reckless fellow, but I should hardly have supposed he would attempt to draw a knife on you."

"I was a little too quick for him, but his intentions were good," said Quint, with a smile.

"Instead of getting out his knife, my partner tripped him so suddenly that he pulled out this, and dropped it," said Cliff, exhibiting the name-plate. "I picked it up afterward, and that's the way I came to know who was the real owner of the dog."

"That certainly resembles my name!" laughed the showman. After a little further talk with the boys,

IN THE CIRCUS TENT.

mainly about the frequent selling of the dog, he asked:
"Have you seen any of his tricks?"

"Winslow showed us some of them," replied Cliff, "and
I made him perform them afterward."

"Did he show you this? Take hold of that end of the
cord."

It was the cord which another attendant (Dick had disappeared) took from Sparkler's collar. Cliff held one end
of it, the showman swung it by the other end, and at a
word the dog, running in, began to jump the rope with
surprising ease and gracefulness.

"I wish I had known he could do that!" Cliff exclaimed
admiringly. "Would n't it have pleased our folks?"—
turning to Quint, who smiled amused assent.

"Here 's another very pretty performance."

The showman tossed aside the cord, and reached for a
drum brought by the attendant. He requested Cliff to
hold one side of it, while he held the other, facing him,
and raising the drum about three feet from the ground.
At a word, Sparkler made a swift dash, and leaped straight
through it, bursting both drumheads, with a double ex-
plosion, and landing on the turf beyond. The drumheads,
as the boys perceived, were of paper.

"That makes me feel bad!" Quint remarked, while
Cliff was expressing his unbounded admiration.

"How so?" Mr. Barnum asked, as he tossed the broken
drum to the attendant.

"To think any other owner for that dog has turned up,

and that he does n't belong to my partner," Quint replied,
with a humor the showman appreciated.

Mr. Barnum asked the boys a few questions about their
adventure, and laughed heartily at the amusing parts of
it. He then said:

"Have you seen a notice of the reward offered? I am
having it posted now with the show-bills, and I 've had it
sent to a few country papers."

"I have n't seen it," Cliff replied; "I don't know anything
about any reward, except what you said in your telegram."

Mr. Barnum was opening a long, well-filled pocket-book.

"I offered a moderate sum—forty dollars. Then, there
are your expenses. Of course I meant your expenses
bringing the dog from Biddicut; but I think, with all the
trouble you 've had, I ought to allow ten dollars on that
account. Then, there 's the money you paid for the dog
—ten dollars more. Besides, there are two of you; and
I am glad to get King Francis back at any price. How 's
this? Satisfactory?" And he put into Cliff's hand six
ten-dollar bank-notes.

"Oh, Mr. Barnum!" Cliff exclaimed, completely over-
come by such unexpected munificence. "Forty dollars is
enough—more than we expected! You need n't say
anything about the expenses. And I forgot—I meant to
tell you—Winslow gave me back *that* ten dollars."

"So much the better!" said the showman, smiling in
hearty enjoyment of the surprise and pleasure he was able
to afford two such honest-minded youths. "It is thirty
dollars apiece. I think you have earned it, and if you are

the sort of boys I take you for, a little nest-egg like that is n't going to do you any harm."

"It 's a small fortune to us!" said Cliff, with glistening eyes. "Here, Quint, you must take charge of your share"—dividing the money on the spot. "I am afraid to have so much money about me!"

"Well, thanks! and good fortune to you!" said the showman, holding out both hands to the boys.

"Oh, *we* thank *you*, Mr. Barnum—I can't tell you how much!" replied Cliff. "I suppose I must say good-by to Sparkler, too; that 's the only thing I am sorry for now. Sparkler is n't his name?" he said, looking up, as he gave the dog a parting caress.

"King Francis is the only name we know him by." Mr. Barnum then said: "Did you ever see my show?"

"Never; but we have always wanted to," said Cliff, with shining eyes.

The attendant who had carried the drum away now returned with two packages looking like books in wrappers. Mr. Barnum said, as he took them:

"Show these young men to the best reserved seats there are left." Then, presenting one of the packages to each of the boys: "This is the story of my life. I hope you will find it instructive, and that your interest in it will not be lessened by the fact that you have seen and talked with the writer."

"I have heard of your book," said Cliff, "and I know we shall be interested in it, and think all the more of it because you gave it to us!" He was stammering his thanks, when Quint in a low voice said something in his ear, which the showman overheard.

"Write my autograph in the books? Certainly, if you wish it. Go to your places now, and I will send them around to you before the show is over."

The proud parade of the Roman Hippodrome, with its horses and chariots and solemn elephants, gaudy banners and braying trumpets, was beginning its stately circuit of the arena when the boys reëntered the great tent. Then, as they mounted to the places to which the attendant guided them, with opulence in their pockets and exultation in their hearts, the sonorous brazen measures of the band burst forth, rivaling in sound the majestic movement and gorgeous colors of the pompous procession.

"Is n't this grand!" said Cliff, his face shining as with the light of victory.

"It 's judgmatical!" replied Quint, with a high and haughty smile.

www.ingramcontent.com/pod-product-compliance
Lightning Source LLC
Chambersburg PA
CBHW020852020726
47497CB00005B/1371